Bryan Walpert is the author of a short story collection, *Ephraim's Eyes*; the poetry collections *Etymology, A History of Glass*, and most recently *Native Bird*; and the scholarly books *Poetry and Mindfulness: Interruption to a Journey* and *Resistance to Science in Contemporary American Poetry*. His work has been recognized by the Royal Society of New Zealand Manhire Award in Creative Science Writing-Fiction, the Montreal International Poetry Award, the New Zealand Poetry Society International Poetry Competition and the James Wright Poetry Award (U.S.). He is a Professor in creative writing at Massey University in Auckland. More on Bryan can be found at bryanwalpert.com.

For Nancy

First published in Seizure by Brio Books in 2020

Brio Books

PO Box Q324, QVB Post Office,

NSW 1230, Australia

www.seizureonline.com
www.briobooks.com.au

Cataloguing-in-publication data is available from the National Library of Australia

978-1-922267-23-8 (print)

978-1-922267-24-5 (digital)

Internal design and typesetting © Brio Books 2020

Cover illustration and design by Sam Paine,
www.sampaine.com

Edited by Alice Grundy

LATE SONATA

BRYAN WALPERT

Songful, with the most intimate feeling.

ONE

Basically, when Michael died, my wife gave up being my wife. She gave up being Talia. She'd been the toughest person I'd ever known close up, certainly tougher than me. She could have fought it longer if she'd had the will. I want to say that overnight she grew smaller. I suppose she simply became the physical size she'd always been, that whatever projection of personality keeps us looking alive, bigger than who we are, had vanished, air out of a balloon. In the morning, she was old, frail, in need of true assistance for the first time. And she left me on my own. She had an escape, her declining faculties, her Alzheimer's, and she embraced it, took that back door, left me in the too-large house of memory. Small wonder I write my own escapes.

Listen to Beethoven's Sonata No. 30 in E Major, Op. 109. Really listen to it. Not while you're cooking or ironing or reading or paying the bills. Listen with your eyes closed. Lie down on the rug. If you can, listen beside someone you love, while they are still capable of sharing it. Give your attention to every note, every silence. I've sought out so many versions. Old phonograph records, CDs, online. What is it is about that piece that makes it impossible to hate, impossible not to love, even though it is the very thing with which my wife, when she was whole, betrayed me? Betrays me still.

I wake to a noise.

For a moment I remain in bed, listening for further sounds, wondering if it was in my head, the noise part of a dream. I try to recall the details which slip into the corners of the room. Then the world to which I do not want to return returns. I lie there just a moment, gathering the energy to get up, to make sure Talia has not escaped into a darkness deeper and more dangerous than the one she inhabits during her waking hours.

I am surprised, as I still am every time I wake, to find myself in Michael's old bedroom, lying on his soft double bed that replaced the cot when he was two and a half and whose mattress we replaced once more with this one when he was ten. Though it is too dark to see it now, I know this room still shows signs of the teenager who left for university. We've made a few adjustments to make it comfortable for the occasional guest, Talia's sister or one of her colleagues who might come into town en route to a conference. Not that we get too many guests anymore given her sister is dealing with her own health issues and Talia's now complete absence from any work-related activities. Michael himself would stay here, of course, when he used to visit for a couple of nights. We eventually took down some of the posters — Michael once joked that it wasn't necessary to preserve history — and put some of his personal effects in drawers. But the framed photograph of Michael playing a concert at the local church when he was thirteen remains on the dresser. The piano trophies and awards still sit on the shelves, alongside his old books. I should give at least the books away. Some day.

I've spent too long in bed. It's quiet now, which portends worse than the banging I heard before. When Michael called out as a baby, it was Talia who got up in the wee hours. I throw on my robe and slippers, leave Michael's room, turn on the hall light. As I walk down the stairs, I can see a light on in the kitchen, but when I arrive Talia is not there. The fridge door is ajar, a glass half-filled with orange juice on the counter. A pot that I'd used and left by the sink lies on the floor.

Talia. I say it softly, then louder.

The familiar panic flutters in my chest. I'd lain there for only a few moments, but I should have jumped out of bed immediately.

I walk into the living room, shadows cast by the light coming from the kitchen. I try to imagine where she has gone. The front door is closed, the security chain hooked. I walk toward the basement door. I take deep breaths as I descend the steep stairway, try to think through the steps I need to take. The door from the basement to the backyard, where the woods lie beyond, is ajar, the air cooling the room. Or is it the heat leaving the room. Stupid thing to be thinking now.

I walk out onto the grass, my slippers immediately damp. I look carefully, but the moon, though nearly full, is covered by clouds. I should have brought the torch with me, but I hesitate to take the time to run inside to get it. It would give her time to go farther afield.

Talia?

I turn to the patio, thinking perhaps she is in one of the chairs, will her to be sitting in one, wholly oblivious of my calls, but they are empty. With little choice, I run back into the house, into the kitchen, my wet slippers squishing on the linoleum, where I find the torch after fumbling in the drawer, then return outside. I shift its feeble spot around the yard, then head toward the woods at the edge of our property. My wife is lost somewhere, as she is almost everywhere — and I with her.

What I am investigating, what I want to know, is who slept with my wife. It is an odd question to return to now, decades later when it should hardly matter. I would have thought that after so many years I'd be more dispassionate about it. But that isn't how the mind works, or the heart. I want to know who fucked my wife.

I don't have it in me to raise it again with Talia, not that she could be guaranteed to remember. Talia sometimes knows who I am, though less and less. More often she remembers Michael. For her, our son is sometimes still in the next room, still a child who might be coaxed to the keyboard. But she's now the child who must be coaxed to take her medication. She never speaks of the injury she inflicted on me. Unlike her, I've no recourse to forgetfulness, and I have no one left to tell it to. My memory of her betrayal so many years ago has become fresh again with a new discovery, drawn from the pages of my wife's completed manuscript, the last thing she will ever write: a book on her beloved Beethoven's sonatas. When she began to deteriorate, I promised her I would edit it, would erase from the text all traces of her growing illness, and even if most of the time she does not remember that promise, I carry on. Halfway through, there is so much I now wish I didn't know about the sonata. Everything I know of its form, if it can be said to have one, everything of its history, every detail engraved now in my brain is a detail hard won by my wife's illness. The same illness erasing the very knowledge she left on the pages in front of me, even as I learn more about her than I thought there could be left to discover, things that might have, should have, remained buried.

If her memories of our life come and go, Talia somehow still remembers how to play. Her hands, if I place them on the keys, can still bring from her baby grand the beauty of one of Beethoven's late sonatas, its rage and requiem. It centres her. In truth, I do this as much for myself as for her. For those few moments, she is my wife again. Maybe it shows a weakness of character — lord knows, I have many weaknesses — but this is what I do: Once she begins, when she is so focused she hardly notices I'm there, I step outside to the front lawn to watch through the living room window as she plays. From there, I see the back of her head, her hands moving. I wonder what our neighbours think of this — new neighbours, there less than a year, with none of the shared history that forgives idiosyncrasies; I wonder whether they notice me standing as long as I can in my own front yard, even as darkness falls, peering through the living room window like a curious stranger. From the other side of the glass, she is the girl I saw through another window play piano at a party forty years ago. You know what I mean — yesterday.

Talia's betrayal, never forgotten but so long buried that I could imagine it forgotten, has returned fresh to me thanks to a simple notation she made in a margin in her manuscript. Talia is nothing if not meticulous in her research. Or was. I've always admired the precision not just in her language but in the level of detail, the care with which she cites sources, the depths to which she goes to support every point. It was this very meticulousness, in the end, that led me to return to her affair and to consider which lies it might have begotten.

Along the way in her manuscript, on p. 187, it

hardly surprised me to find a note in brackets to herself. I found many of these. This one sat in a lengthy passage in a chapter devoted to Op. 109. It said 'check op. cit., 109 file.' At the time, I thought she must not have had time to do this before she had to abandon the work, before it became too difficult for her to remember, to concentrate. I try to imagine how that must have felt to her. Talia is the one who remembered birthdays, phone numbers, passwords. She remembered my own mother's birthday more often than I did, all those years ago, had her nephews' birthdays (and birth weights, though I could hardly see this as useful) on instant recall. What did it feel like to find an empty space where the date of a composition should be, or the name of Beethoven's birthplace, or the key of a sonata she'd played many times (never mind the physical keys to the house)? How often had she had to double-check a fact, only to forget whether she had double-checked it and have to do it again? What private systems had she developed — she'd never told me — to remind herself of what she had or hadn't done in the manuscript, and how much time had the scaffolding that she'd needed to create to maintain the edifice of her intellect detracted from progress on the project itself?

She crossed out any number of notes of this sort, a clean single line through the words to indicate, no doubt, that she had taken care of it. This one remained untouched. It's possible, even likely, that she'd already double-checked this citation, that her failure to cross it off was a mark merely of her own growing uncertainty. But I owed it to her to be sure. To check meant opening Talia's filing cabinets. These are in the office that was once mine but that some years back we began to share. I felt as though I were invading the depths of her privacy. It helped that Talia was out with Anna, who had taken her to the park for an hour's walk, as she does a few times a week to give us both a break and perhaps for herself, too, what with her husband, Geoff, also gone.

Talia has always loved Anna. It is hard not to. She'd always been a great foil for Geoff. If for Geoff life was a good wave he could surf, Anna made it possible. She has always made sure the bank accounts were full, the bills paid, the mortgage refinanced, arranged the will. But she did these things seemingly without resentment, though she had her own career to deal with, her own ambitions as an historian, an academic. How she balanced all of these things with Geoff so often in the lab remains a mystery to me. Anna was Talia's closest friend for thirty years, someone Talia took to immediately, though they are so very different. Talia, tall, fair, redhead; Anna, petite, olive-skinned, brunette. Where Talia is sarcastic, Anna is sincere. Where Talia is incisive, her mind by its nature one that makes distinctions and distinctions within distinctions, Anna sees the world — though just as intelligently — with a sense of pleasure in its ambiguities.

In all of our years together, I had never dared to look through Talia's filing cabinets. When I opened the drawers, I was not surprised to find them meticulously — and neatly — labelled and organised. She had two drawers devoted solely to Beethoven, a section on the sonatas (from last to first, going from front to back), a thick file on Op. 109. My own filing cabinet, while not in disarray, is far less organised. There are often too many folders in a drawer, too many files crammed into a single hanging folder, so that I have to pull hard to extract one and dig with my hand to make space to reinsert it. But hers are arranged with much more care. The drawers are full, but not packed. It's a simple matter to slip the file from the drawer, which closes easily (mine tend to get stuck).

I brought the Op. 109 file back to the kitchen table, placed it beside the laptop. Before digging in, I felt the need to be braced by some coffee. Michael's French press. Why do we keep these reminders of the past? When we took that trip to see Michael and Jacob in New York a couple of years ago, they took us to breakfast at a bistro, far nicer than I'd expected, far more upscale than called for by breakfast. I wondered whether Michael was trying to impress us, or whether — I suppose this is more likely — this was simply his life now, a life of greater sophistication, greater expense, than ours. Even at breakfast, the tables were covered in white linens. We were served coffee in individual-sized French presses. We must have expressed some pleasure in those miniature presses because when we left a couple of days later, Michael presented us with two of them as a parting gift. Since then, we'd often used those instead of drip coffee. They sit side by side in the cupboard. I extracted one of them, scooped in the coffee (Michael and Jacob, extolling the virtues of fresh coffee, would grind their beans each time, but

I can't be bothered and, heathen that I am, simply buy pre-ground at the supermarket, whatever brand is on sale), then put the kettle on.

While the water boiled, I opened the file and started searching through the notes, copies of source pages, bibliography lists. There were a few full articles she'd printed or copied from journals, a few newspaper clippings — a review of a recent recording, for example. Everything was clearly marked in her handwriting with a comment ('cf. Deanna's article, 2002') or question ('can this be the right date?'). I found the article she reminded herself to double-check fairly deep in the file; she'd copied the entire thing. I lifted it out. Beneath it sat a folded piece of paper, with her name on it, in handwriting that was not hers.

I shouldn't have explored further. Not just because it's none of my business — it's her file, I reminded myself, and I'm in it only to take care of a single task — but because I sensed trouble. How many factors go into that state of mind we call intuition? The fact that it stood out from the other papers in its texture, that someone else's handwriting had formed her name, that it was folded in half. Other things I didn't consciously notice, too, probably together formed some sort of impression taken in by a part of my brain working behind the scenes. I hesitated.

Still, as I said, I am a man of many weaknesses. I took the paper from the file and unfolded it. The page had started to stiffen but was not yet brittle, a piece of stationery from Hotel Gerrard, one of those grand hotels from the 1940s that has managed to stay the course with renovations and new management now and again, retaining its essential character, with its tall, ornate ceilings and large armchairs, though a bit rough around the gilded edges. It had the look of a man's handwriting. And, yes, I read it. Even all these years later, it was hard to read all of the things he wrote that I tended not to tell her, tended in my naiveté to believe, because she was so strong and acerbic, that she didn't need to hear. But what was most concerning, and the reason I suppose that she'd hidden the page deep in the file on Op. 109, was that the letter refers to watching her play that sonata. The letter is undated. But I remember the concert he was referring to, one that I didn't attend, at the university. I thought I couldn't attend. I was deep in my own work, was on a roll, asked her to understand. I was young enough to think she could.

That concert took place about a year after her affair had ended, or when she claimed it had ended. Had they continued the entire time — and beyond? Or had they found one another again, briefly? I was interested, as if from a great distance, to see that my hand shook as I read it a second time. The concert had taken place in February. Michael was born the following November. How can something as simple as arithmetic change the way you think about your life? How long had they been going to Hotel Gerrard?

Ah, but my escapes. Once, as I was reorganising my bookshelves, she pointed to my novels lined up on a new shelf and said, 'A resolution to every dilemma.' I knew what she meant. Each was predicated on what at the time seemed an irresolvable problem in my life — professional, personal. I didn't take particular care to cover my autobiographical tracks. But each veered from reality in a way I didn't expect. Though each in some way offered some sort of emotional relief — 'wish fulfilments,' Talia used to call my books, or once or twice, 'your little redemptions' — it always took a different turn than I might have predicted when I began. Part true, part speculative, the books I wrote offered me emotional gifts, pathways I hadn't taken or couldn't take. But each was like the gift of a genie in those old stories, who gives you exactly what you ask for but in a way you could not have predicted and, perhaps, might not have chosen. For example, during a very difficult financial year — Talia was on a year's maternity leave without pay after Michael was born, I was between book projects, and half of my normal freelance editing had not come through, so we were struggling to live on what I could scrape together and some savings — I wrote a novel in which a writer-protagonist in similar straits receives a bequest from a deceased and long-forgotten great aunt (of course there were strings attached, including the sale of an unusual house designed by the aunt, which led to family discoveries and tensions). While starting another book, Michael took quite ill with a challenging to diagnose condition; in the book, the protagonist's son needs a transfusion of an extraordinarily rare blood type prior to a bone marrow transplant; the protagonist discovers an unknown third cousin who in the end provides the needed blood (in reality, Michael, fifteen at the time, didn't need that solution, though for a few frightening weeks we didn't know what would happen). In each case, I tended to find a sort of architecture to help give a framework to the book. In *Bequest*, for instance, the aunt was literally an architect, and the book was structured as a series of rooms — each major event involved a room in her house — with interruptive 'corridor' passages voiced by the house itself. In *Blood Type*, the book followed an improvised three-part cellular structure. *Your little redemptions*, Talia once said in her dry fashion, *do tend toward an experimental formulism*.

Still, Talia understood, I think, even as she mocked me. Her Beethoven put his life into his music — the pain of his failed love affairs, his growing deafness, his battle for custody of his nephew Karl and then Karl's unsuccessful suicide attempt. It didn't surprise me that once her diagnosis was undeniable she said, *I suppose you'll want to write through this, Stephen*. It seemed to me, though we did not discuss it, less observation than a form of permission. But it was too soon, too urgent. Then Michael died. I couldn't take her advice — wasn't ready. Still, if I couldn't write something so close to home, writing remained my escape, just the simple act of it. It's just that this time, I thought, the story had to be far from home, far from my own life, a way to look outward rather than inward. So for the first time I thought I would try something truly speculative. The idea was based on some research that had come out about ageing, which was something of an interest at my own age. I saw something first in the newspaper about a trial, a potential move in the direction of reversing the effects of ageing. Then I read something similar in *Scientific American*, which I'd picked up on impulse, as I sometimes do. So without any expectation, I began a book tentatively called *Young, Again.* The protagonist has lost his wife. There is no son — I couldn't go there. It's a fantasy — any ageing man's fantasy — but it seemed like something I could enjoy exploring, something to help me forget, if only briefly. As I said, I have many weaknesses.

So when not editing her book, I indulge myself in a bit of escape by working on my own. Two hours each day, the first two hours in the morning, while Talia is still asleep. When in a good rhythm, my habit has always been to work six days, then have Sundays off. On the other hand, I can go months without writing a word. This is always the way it has been, from the first novel. Eventually, no matter how long it takes, I settle into a pattern of a thousand words a day. *When I'm disciplined, I'm disciplined,* I used to tell friends, *and when I'm not, I'm not. In other words,* Talia used to say to them, rolling her eyes, *he's not disciplined.* Still, she read every book, two times: once in draft to give it a critical eye, once when it was published, then never again. She has a copy of each, signed by the author (she enjoyed observing that my signature on novel nine, published two years ago, was noticeably shakier than novel one which was published seven years after we were married). Her copies are lined up on her bookshelf in the bedroom, along with a hundred other books by various authors on an eclectic mix of subjects. Her bookshelf on the right side of the room, mine on the left, twin histories of our hearts.

The book is about a man in his seventies who undergoes experimental treatment designed to improve bone density and palliate some other symptoms of ageing, including memory, as well as experimental treatment meant to lengthen telomeres, the chromosomes whose gradual shortening is in part responsible for the effects of ageing. His name, in the working draft, is Orville because it strikes me as a name you can imagine as elderly but can also imagine to fit a man in his prime, many years ago. Perhaps, though, it is too old-fashioned. The book takes place in the near future. Orville is recently retired from a career in investigative work for corporate and private clients but one of his acquaintances, Alex, about fifteen years his junior, is a researcher whose lab at the university is at the forefront of such experimental techniques designed to ease the effects of age. Until recently, these were used on rats. The lab began a small-scale human study in partnership with a pharmaceuticals company. Orville managed to work his way into that trial. He surprised himself by lying on his form about his recent health. One of the requirements was that he not be currently suffering from cancer or in remission; Orville was in remission, something Alex did not know, as Orville had kept it quiet, as had his doctor, an old friend Orville called upon to give him a clean bill of health and who did so with great hesitation, only because of his long friendship with Orville and his own imminent retirement.

The drug trial takes place at a clinic in the medical school, about three miles from Orville's house. A week after he learns he has been accepted for the trial, Orville rides his bike to the clinic. It's mainly flat on the way there, with a small hill near the end. He took up biking a few years earlier, along with a gym membership, an attempt to stay fit in body and mind. He locks it in the bike area — an advantage of the campus is that it accommodates bikes everywhere — then walks in from the July heat and humidity to a blast of cold air in the lobby, which is small but not cramped. He gives his name to the young receptionist who wears headphones over one lovely ear as she types.

Orville can't tell whether she is on the phone, whether it is safe or polite to speak with her. Etiquette, he thinks, is always a step behind technology, though the young are always more attuned to the technology, the old to the etiquette. She looks at him briefly, holds up an index finger, the universal sign for *Wait, there is someone more important than you because they are on the phone and you are merely in front me.* That answers that.

She must be in her mid-twenties. He takes a moment to admire — at his age, it is all one can realistically hope for, though still the heart scoffs at realism — the smooth line of her neck, the fullness of her lips, the care with which she has only lightly applied makeup, the slight downward turn of her nose. The nose is an imperfection that must worry her unnecessarily. Women in their twenties have no realistic idea how beautiful they are. They are taken to magnifying minor blemishes into the major issues they're not — and she is above average. She has her hair — black, though surely it is not a natural colour — to her shoulders, wears a headband that makes the earpiece sit awkwardly. Rebecca — it's on her name tag — barely looks up as she types, then smiles with her mouth only, asks for his name.

Orville Scott. For the trial.

She hands over a clipboard of forms, gestures to the seats even as her eyes return to the screen. Beyond the desk are four rows of chairs, a coffee table with magazines, some posters on the walls promoting mammograms, touting breastfeeding and flu vaccines, the latter a hold-over from the previous winter or perhaps the one before that.

Plenty of seats. He finds one by the magazines, fills out the paperwork. Other than a confidentiality form, most of the information he'd already given when he'd applied to join. Typical. But he dutifully provides the details again and returns it to Rebecca, who thanks him without really seeing him. Then back to his seat and a *People* magazine. It's less to read than for camouflage, so he can look around. A young mother, pregnant, reading to a girl, about two, who keeps touching her pigtails. A middle-aged woman in a slim-cut navy suit, on break from the office — an executive, perhaps, or lawyer — reading something on her phone.

After a few minutes, an older man, somewhere around Orville's age, goes through the routine with Rebecca, sits a few chairs over. After a few minutes, he turns to Orville.

Here for the trial? the man asks.

How'd you guess?

You're an old man.

Right back at you. Orville. He sticks out a hand.

Reginald. Reg.

Reg moves over a seat so there's only one between them. He has most of his hair, silvered, carefully brushed. He'd shaven meticulously, except for a closely cropped grey Van Dyke. He smells pleasantly of cologne, wears a ring on his pinkie, has broad shoulders beneath a button down short-sleeve shirt that reveals muscles but also a paunch. He wears khaki shorts, leather sandals.

Orville says, Looking to feel a bit younger and stronger?

I could use the income.

Hate to break it to you, Reg, but they're not paying us.

No kidding. I was a plumber. Getting a little hard crawling into tight spaces. Arthritis and the rest. I'd still be doing it part-time if it didn't hurt so much.

Wait a minute, Orville says. What's your last name.

Shannon.

I think you came to my house. Must be twenty years ago. You put in a water filter.

Reg looks at Orville more carefully. I don't know, he says. Wouldn't surprise me.

So you'd get back into plumbing? Right back into the old life?

Sure, why not? I liked it. I was damn good at it, ran my own business. I mean, I was happy to retire at first. Figured I'd play my guitar, read, travel, do the

house projects I'd always put off because I was too busy
fixing other people's problems.

Have you?

Sure. Some, anyway. But that's getting old. So to
speak. Then, as I say, there's the money. Savings isn't
going as far as I thought it would.

I hear you.

The nurse, standing at the double-doors to the
examination rooms, interrupts them: Orville Scott?

Go get 'em, Reg says, you're looking a bit past your
peak.

I find Talia not far into the woods, sitting on the
ground, her back against a tree. Her arms are around
her knees.

Talia, it's Stephen.

Stephen.

A rush of gratitude, of relief. She knows who I am,
which will make it easier for the moment. I link my
arm through hers, take her back through the yard, but
she pulls me toward the patio, sits in one of the woven
chairs, in her nightgown. She's sitting at the very edge
of the chair, her hands tightly in her lap, looking out
over the creek that runs between our yard and our
neighbour's, visible in the light of the moon now that
the clouds have shifted.

I go back inside to get a blanket from the couch and
put it on top of her, gently encourage her to sit back
in the chair. I pull the other chair beside her. In the
pale light, I can see her hair is undone, loose around

her face. When I take her hand, it's cold, so I rub it between mine.

The stars, she says. We should take them off.

With the clouds dispersing, I recognise Orion's Belt, the Big Dipper. One of the things we've always liked about this house, outside of our little town of Lyons, about twenty minutes from Boulder, Colorado, is an array of stars we can see on clear nights. Not as many as we could see thirty years ago, of course, but still it's beautiful.

Take them off?

It's like holding onto his childhood. We shouldn't do that.

I understand, then, that she means the stars on Michael's ceiling. I moved out of our bedroom three months ago into Michael's, to give each of us space. She has disturbed sleep, with groans and noises she never used to make. She moves a lot. I felt guilty leaving her in the room, as though I were abandoning her to her illness, so held off for a long time. I was exhausted during the day as a result of all the disturbances — it brought back the years when Michael was a baby and refused to sleep through the night. It was Anna who finally gave me the emotional permission to sleep in another room. *It doesn't do either of you any good if you're exhausted or resentful of Talia*, Anna had said. She asked, knowing the answer, whether Talia would be so sentimental if the situation were reversed.

Except for some hard moments in our marriage, when I'd spent a few nights or in one or two cases a couple of weeks on the couch, we'd shared that bedroom for going on thirty-five years, as long as we'd been in this house. Good years, mostly. Watching the storms roll in from the deck, shiraz in our hands. Listening to music together, as she taught me how to *really* listen. Coming to my computer to work on a book to find a yellow Post-It with a musical note drawn on its stave, a signal to get up and look for others on the door frame, the hallway, a trail of notes on notes, as she called them, letters to decode, given the small proportion of the alphabet they represented: d-e-b unscrambled to b-e-d (to which I would hurriedly scoot finding her within), f-e-e-d (a less hurried but still encouraged walk to the kitchen, where she had prepared something special), the more obscure d-e-c (I kept thinking *December?* but worked out she meant to meet her on the deck) or the baffling e-e-c (I gave up — turned out this was a faux-exclamation to alert me we had finally caught a troublesome mouse in a trap I'd set and reset for a week, a nuisance it was my job to remove). We moved to this house when Michael was a baby, from an apartment across town. While he napped, we painted our room deep blue because a bedroom, Talia said, should have the colour of peace, should induce calm, restfulness. We slept out in the living room while we were painting it, Michael beside us in his bassinet. Then we painted his room. For that Talia chose a lighter blue with white trim near the ceiling, around the windows. We moved him in initially when he was five months old, into a full-size cot. Until then, his bassinet was by our bed.

At some point — he was ten or eleven — we'd gone

a couple of hours to the city to see a combined space/ classical music show at the new planetarium. At the shop — they had us exit through the gift shop, for reasons that became obvious — he'd asked us to buy a pack of glow-in-the dark stars, the kind that stick to the ceiling. They came with a star chart, some explanations of the constellations. We were not indulgent parents, and not spontaneous purchasers, but Talia gave me a nod. That day and for the next week, he stood on his desk chair and meticulously arranged them on the ceiling, looking down at the star chart unfolded — it was huge — on his bed. The first evening I moved into Michael's room, I'd spent a couple of hours in bed, the light on, reading. When I turned out the light and lay down, the stars were a glowing explosion over the bed. I had forgotten.

Anyway, Talia says, they must disturb you.

I'll take care of it if you want me to, I say. But it's not necessary on my account. I like them.

Talia says nothing.

I ask, Do you want to go back to bed?

She stares at the portion of creek visible from our patio, the water glinting in the moonlight. I go back inside for a second blanket. When I return to my seat, I take her hand again and look up at the sky, at the depth of the stars, until I realise I've slept and they are gone. Talia is still asleep, her head tilted back, snoring. I'm stiff, cold. It's day, a drizzle rippling the creek, the sky grey with morning.

And our friend Orville? The treatment itself proves easy enough. As they had explained during an orientation, he sits in an easy chair, an IV in his right arm, a bottle of water by his left. He reads magazines for an hour.

The nurse, probably in her mid-thirties, though it was getting harder to estimate age accurately now that everyone looked so young, comes in and out of the room throughout that hour, checking on him, smiling. Any odd sensations? she asks now and again.

Am I supposed to feel something?

She shakes her head. No, of course not. Do you?

She takes vitals a few times, jotting them down. The supervising researcher comes through, a doctor in his early fifties, his hair nearly grey, but thick and full. He is thin and fit in a polo shirt visible beneath the white coat, which seems wholly unnecessary, a sort of prop meant to inspire confidence. He speaks louder than necessary, the sort of overly cheerful bombast that is meant to reassure, to suggest nothing happening is a big deal — what passes as bedside manner. Orville remembers it from his cancer treatments. Different doctor, same voice.

You might feel a bit tired today, Orville, he says.

The doctor is not quite old enough to call Orville by his first name. If you do, the doctor continues, don't worry about it. Just get some rest. Give a us call if you're not feeling better by this time tomorrow.

He feels fine as he bikes back to the house. He takes the long way home, a circuitous route that includes a challenging uphill climb. It is a habit he developed coming back from this part of the city during his wife's last years. About two years before Gina died, during a period of remission for her, they started biking together and would often ride to the university, where they would go to the gym or enjoy some of the long meandering paths through the large campus, studded with tall trees. The short way home, across a large city park, took them past a skate park, which had become a hangout not just for kids, but increasingly for men in their twenties who carried decrepit backpacks and dirty rolled-up sleeping bags, men who looked like they hadn't showered in days and asked, often aggressively, for money. Orville and Gina ignored the shouts that followed them, the pleas for spare change. Once, though, as they'd ridden past, one of the men — he wore a baseball cap backwards, Orville remembered, and had a wispy moustache and goatee — had said *Bitch*, and reached out and swatted Gina's back wheel, Orville directly behind her. Gina had wobbled, then stopped, catching herself with her foot. Orville stopped, too, got off his bike and walked up to Gina to make sure she was okay. She'd been feeling weak that day, for several days in fact, and neither of them wanted to admit that her remission was coming to an end. Baseball Cap approached them.

That got your attention, didn't it? he said.

Orville ignored him. Gina said she was fine, not to worry about it.

She's fine, man, you heard her, Baseball Cap said.

No thanks to you, Orville said.

Orville, don't, Gina said.

You better listen to her, *Orville*, Baseball Cap said.

Maybe you'd better leave us alone.

Baseball Cap said, Maybe you should put a crowbar in your wallet and give me twenty dollars.

I don't think so.

Baseball Cap pushed Orville hard in the chest so that Orville fell over his own bike, which he'd left lying on the grass. He found himself on his back, the grass wet, the smell of dirt. It had been decades since an interaction like this. He didn't feel so much afraid as ridiculous.

Baseball Cap stood over him. Twenty dollars is the price of passage this way.

Gina said, Orville, please just give him what you have.

By now, five or six of the other young men were standing behind Baseball Cap, who looked around him, aware of his audience. Orville knew at this point that the guy would never let it go, that it had become a point of pride. He looked at Gina, who seemed on the verge of tears.

Orville stood up, took out his wallet and gave him a ten and a five. He said, this is what I have.

Baseball Cap took it. Next time you come by, remember you owe me five.

That was the last time they rode through the park, and since Gina's death, Orville hasn't been able to face going through it again.

While Talia naps, in the bedroom, I look at the two photographs taken a quarter-century apart, side by side on top of the piano. In both, our son Michael is sitting at this same piano bench. One was taken when he was eight years old. The other was taken a year ago, the last time Michael came home. He had just turned thirty-four. In the most recent photo, he is wearing a camel sports jacket with jeans, a light blue shirt open at the neck. His hair, which he sometimes allowed to grow curly and bushy, is close-cropped, with a few strands of early silver. A concert pianist, Michael took his mother's ambitions and ran with them. Sometimes when he played for us in the living room I could see him as a person apart, an individual in the world, a man suddenly disconnected from the many frames of memories that normally make it so difficult to disentangle an image in the present from those of the past: For that instant, he is simply a man with the start of grey at the temples, a nose that still holds evidence of a break in childhood, a strong chin with a day's stubble. I see him with enough distance to appreciate that there is a professional pianist playing us a private concert, that hundreds of people pay substantial amounts of money for a much less intimate pleasure. As much as I have always loved hearing him and his mother play together, is it a life any father would choose for a son? So intensely competitive, so much travel. But I can't recall a single complaint from Michael. A year since his feet have crossed our threshold, but he still can't wholly elude me. The world doesn't permit for that anymore: I torture myself, late at night when I can't sleep, with internet clips from Michael's concerts or from television interviews.

Michael used to come home regularly. He'd find ways to detour after one of his concert dates, would suddenly knock at the door. *It's your house*, Talia would say, *you can come in anytime*. Michael would say, *I wouldn't want to surprise you*. As though he might catch his parents in the lounge *in flagrante delicto*. She misses him terribly. I do, too, though he's always been closer to his mother. They've had the piano between them, literally and figuratively, and I could barely pick out a tune. She was his first teacher. As good as Talia was, though, she knew when he had moved beyond what she could teach him. Talia had once held hopes for a concert career herself. As with all things in her life, when that didn't happen she dealt with it pragmatically. She returned to graduate school, got her doctorate in music history and theory and has been satisfied with playing the occasional local or regional concert. All of her true concert ambitions went into Michael. Not that she was a stage mother. She knew when to let go, knew it was best to let him find his own ambitions, which he obligingly did, to her public pride and, because it took him so far away so often, to her private regret.

The strangeness of growing old. How many times I've heard someone say, *But I'm the same person inside as I was when I was eighteen*. I suppose I've said something like that once or twice myself. It's true that sometimes I feel like the person I've always been (I suppose I would realistically peg my internal age to around thirty). But this, as with so many things, surely turns out to be illusory. Our memories are not to be trusted, especially memories of what we were like, how we felt. We look at the past through the lens of who we are now. Every memory is more in the order of interpretation, rather than recollection. Geoff once explained this to me. Geoff, who when we were in our twenties vomited out of the passenger window as I drove his girlfriend's Dodge (drove it because I was slightly less drunk than either of them. Geoff dealt with the encrustation on the outside of the car the next day and her departure a few weeks later). Geoff, who retired just a few years ago a distinguished professor of neuroscience. (Distinguished must be in the eyes of the beholder, Talia said loudly to Geoff's wife, Anna, as the four of us sat on the patio, enjoying the dinner Talia spent the day cooking for Geoff precisely to celebrate that honour). It feels hardly any time has passed since he was so intensively looking for his first position. For a while, when Talia's mind started to decline more severely, he and I would meet for a drink once a week, while Anna stayed with Talia. It was a kindness bestowed by two old friends, our oldest friends. They gave me a few precious hours of respite, a few hours to remember that I am a person, apart from her. Though mostly Geoff and I talked about Talia, about her loss of memory, about our own memories, the way sometimes they can be so hard to catch, like a difficult fish, but at other times descend without warning or desire, like weather or any feeling. They can be enjoyed but not fully trusted. Geoff told me once that each visit to a memory is not just like a different path through the jungle; it's not even the same jungle. It is as much invention as recollection. There are so many pieces of evidence that my inner life has changed as radically as my outer appearance. The things I think about, fret about, the things I value, the way I respond to what others say, the music I prefer.

Music. Damn the mind and its return to the sonata. Better to think about our man Orville, returning home from the clinic. As he rides home from the clinic, Orville thinks about mowing the lawn, which he still does himself and plans to continue doing as long as he can push the thing. He's always done his own lawn and gardens, except when in treatments for cancer — discovered two years after Gina died — and it had pained him then to hear the clunk of the mower pulled out of the truck bed, the buzz as the man (not a boy, as expected, but only a decade younger than him, grey hair visible beyond the bucket hat, which made it all the more difficult to take) pushed the mower up and down the lawn, in patterns that were — he could see from the bedroom window — different from the ones he'd made for decades. As he walks the bike up the path to the porch, he sees the grass is more than a few days past needing a trim. He tries to remember whether the can in the shed has any petrol left.

Staying fit enough to do his own lawn has been reason enough to keep to his gym schedule several days a week, generally about 10 am on Mondays, Wednesdays and Fridays, a time when users are sparse — a few mums, the occasional young person, but mainly geezers like himself. There is almost always space at the weight machines, even though the old guys tend to take long breaks between reps, sitting on the bench, sweating and lost in thought. It's a beautiful gym, with rows and rows of treadmills, ellipticals, stair climbers, a huge, seemingly endless stack of fluffy white towels, newly built rooms for yoga classes, as well as half a floor devoted to weight machines and free weights. Everything in great shape, including the large, clean locker room with strong, hot showers in private, individual stalls, and bottles of mouthwash at the sinks. Often Orville goes home to shower, though, unless he's going somewhere directly after. He's never enjoyed watching the old guys with their wrinkled balls and their guts hanging out, each walking around with a towel slung over his shoulder like he's Adonis on the mountain. There are plenty of mirrors, but, he thinks, we see what we want to see.

But by the time he's finished a cup of coffee, though, it hits him, the dull exhaustion they'd promised, a body ache that drives away any thought of outdoor work. The ache is familiar. It reminds him of the cancer treatment, though not as bad as that and, he has to hope, not as long lasting. A beautiful day, mid-summer, but he needs to lie down. Sitting at the kitchen table, the upstairs bedroom seems suddenly far away. He settles instead on the couch, shucks off his Nikes to stretch out his legs, rests his head on a throw pillow. He grabs an afghan folded nearby.

From this position, he looks around what he can see of the house he bought with his wife nearly forty years before. Since Gina died, he's tried to keep it looking clean and tidy. He's kept all the photographs on the walls, on the side tables. The table beside and slightly behind his head has a single framed photograph. It's dusty. He and Gina, forty years earlier. On a boat, an old friend at the helm — they'd lost touch with that friend, who knows how long ago now — he and Gina with arms around each other. He's wearing a T-shirt and swim trunks; she's in a light blue bikini. That body. He thinks about the first time he saw it, the curves he traced with his hands. He feels guilty, sometimes, filled with desire for his late wife's former body.

It takes three and a half weeks for Orville to get around to mowing his lawn. It has rained steadily for most of that time before clearing up finally, then drying out. And there is the weekly day of fatigue to deal with. To call the lawn unkempt by the time he feels well enough to get to it would be a kindness.

Orville heads to the basement, which is devoted largely to laundry and storage, along with a small workshop area that he hardly has reason to use. He pulls a cord to turn on a bare bulb then, in the shallow light, fills the mower with petrol, pulls the mower up the stairs and gets to work. Only after mowing the yard, then finding he still has the energy to trim the bushes at the driveway, prune the branches of a self-seeded oak, and transplant the lemon tree he'd gotten at the start of the summer to a sunnier part of the yard — a task he'd been wanting to get to for months — does it occur to him he has been working for several hours without the need for a break, that he still doesn't want one.

Talia finished her manuscript on Beethoven's sonatas as her brain's misfirings made it all too clear this
was to be her last book. Even as the text expanded
along the shore of the page, the tide of her dementia
was ebbing away at the edifices she was constructing.
She knew it well in advance. Talia knew the prognosis, understood what the gradual — monthly, then
weekly, then daily — deteriorations meant. Small
ones first, so small they could be overlooked, justi-
fied. Keys in the fridge. Later there were two different
shoes, unnoticed until we were in the car. A tendency
to repeat the same question answered only minutes
earlier. Washing up liquid in the dishwasher, bub-
bles overflowing onto the linoleum, drenching it so
that the entire floor had to be replaced (not before the
insurance company tried to save it by having industrial
fans set up to dry it out). It could happen to anyone,
I'd say to myself after each such incident, could have
been me on a bad day. She was also — had always
been — absent-minded when writing a book or com-
posing a piece of music. And one has to make accom-
modations to the normal changes of age. Classic, I
suppose, the first instinct to distrust one's perceptions,
then to rationalise. Gradually, though, these incidents
began to accumulate, to worsen. She stood in front of
the utility pantry in the kitchen, demanding to know
what I'd done with the bowl for Angus, Michael's dog
twelve-years dead. She looked at the photograph of
our son, the one I took last year as he sat at the piano
in our living room, and asked who this man was.
No, she said, *this is Michael*, pointing to the framed

photo beside it, of the eight-year-old boy he'd been. My response wasn't fast enough, rarely is, to stop the look of confusion, then fear, in her eyes. Some part of her knew that her resistance to the picture of reality I provided was not worth maintaining. When things grew too obvious to ignore, we had late-night discussions about what to do, some of which she would forget in the mornings. Then the MRI. The diagnosis. The prognosis. The counselling. The medication. The waiting rooms, where I looked around at the elderly or not so elderly with their 'caregivers' — the husbands or wives, the daughters or sons, the siblings — and wondered how many years of memories, of children and spouses, of birthday parties and school dances, of romantic disappointments and rain-spoiled days at the beach, were at that moment, in that room, seeping into oblivion. Then came the myriad, unrelenting methods of keeping her whole: mobile phone alarms, kitchen timers, the endless number of yellow sticky notes — drawn from the same drawer she'd kept them for our notes-on-notes game, long abandoned — that she'd written for herself this time and left on doors, refrigerator shelves, clocks, the medicine cabinet mirror, the pillow.

I still stumble on one now and then that she had written for herself, though she is no longer able to compose them, a few still stuck on walls or cabinets, others given in to gravity and fallen behind desks and side tables, written in the wry voice she used even for herself: *Use the toilet; trust me. This is the study; you spend too much time here. The man in bed beside you is your husband, Stephen; you love him, mainly.* I found those stuck to the wall above my dresser beside each other, why there I've no idea. I left them there, a piece of her voice — I press them with my thumb now and again to secure them a while longer when they threaten to peel off into the air. I can't get myself to throw any of them away, as though these little breadcrumbs might be followed back through time to who she was, who I was, whole. *Mainly.*

Even as she declined, Talia spent as much time as she could finishing her book on Beethoven's sonatas. Michael, on a couple of his visits, helped her. He read sections as she was writing them, helped her find things in her notes, made some suggestions about the notations, played selections to explain his take on her arguments. The last time he came, a year ago when I took his photo, Michael sat with Talia for a couple of hours, helping her to sort through her notes, folders piled on the dining room table in some meticulous order I didn't try to understand. I don't know how much of Michael's assistance she truly needed, though I suspect she accepted it largely because she simply enjoyed his presence, his attention. But if Michael knows Beethoven from the inside out, his strength is not writing, never has been. She made me promise to edit the book to ensure a reasonable standard in the case she could no longer count on herself to do it. I said that surely her colleagues could take this on more successfully. She said she wanted me to send it to Frank at Duke and to Eliane in Toronto for a good technical appraisal, but first she wanted to be sure it made sense, was clear, had a basic arc. It had to be of a professional standard before they saw it. She didn't want it to be an embarrassment, though of course both Frank and Eliane, friends for many years, knew about her condition. What could I say? It was the last thing I wanted — and this is the true reason I tried to pass it off onto her colleagues: to avoid reading a book she could no longer understand or remember writing.

Yet this is exactly what I find myself doing a couple of hours most days, with her publisher's deadline approaching in a few months — a publisher who has no idea of her steady decline because I use her email address to respond to his queries. I read her book on the laptop. Out of habit, I make my edits in track changes, as though she will be able to accept or decline them, as she used to do when she asked me to edit her work. As though she would still be capable of the acerbic responses to my grammatical suggestions — sending links to contradictory style guides to underscore the ambiguity of the rules surrounding some comma placement I had queried, as though I had trespassed by doing exactly what she had asked me to do. This morning, I sat with the laptop at the kitchen table. Though I did not want to edit this book, though it is a task as painful as it is necessary, I find I read it more slowly than required. That is the problem: I hate doing it, but at the same time I want it to last. These pages amount to the last time I will hear her speak as her academic self. As I read and typed this afternoon, she sat with her juice in front of her (she could no longer be trusted with hot drinks). She asked what I was working on.

After the fourth week, Orville's post-treatment period of fatigue shortens, grows less intense. He and Reg meet for drinks. The place has been a bar as long as Orville can remember, though it's changed hands and decor several times. It went through a seedy period in the nineties, but it's a sports bar now, the lights too bright, the place too loud, the televisions visible at every angle and therefore unavoidable, the ambience as overly cheerful as the doctor at the clinic. He and Reg sit at a booth, Orville's back to the television. They order beers — Orville has taken to wheat beer recently, and this one arrives with a slice of lemon, for which Reg mocks him (you want an umbrella too?) — then food. Orville orders a blue-cheese burger with a side of fries and slaw.

You find your appetite improving? Reg asks.

Ravenous.

Me, too.

When it arrives, Orville devours the burger. A few weeks before, he might have taken half home.

Good? Reg asks.

Best burger ever. I don't know whether the food is actually this good or whether my taste is just getting sharper.

Me, too, Reg says. Everything tastes better. No, fuller: steak, fish, beer. Even water has taste.

Orville nods. So it isn't his imagination. And it's

not just taste. All of his senses are regaining a sharpness that he was not aware he had lost, sensations that must have dulled gradually over the years without any sense of degradation. Colours are brighter. He can hear the television — a commercial break on ESPN — clearly over the ambient noise of the conversations at tables around him.

Is it meant to be like this? Orville asks.

Reg shrugs. I don't know. I thought it was mainly muscle, bone, and memory. Maybe it all goes together.

Orville excuses himself to go to the restroom. He stands at the urinal, the stream coming not just more readily but faster and stronger than it has in a long time. The improvement in the waterworks has been a welcome surprise. As he washes his hands, he looks closely in the mirror. Still an old man. Still a familiar stranger staring back, thin white hair, mass of wrinkles around the eyes, nose drooping more than it did years ago. He reaches his hand to his throat. Maybe less of a turkey neck. Or is that wishful thinking?

When he returns to the table, Reg has ordered two more beers. As the waitress collects the plates, to Orville's discomfort Reg tells her she has beautiful hands, asks how long she'd been doing this. She says just a few months, that she will be entering nursing school in the autumn.

You can lay those healing hands on me anytime, Reg says with a wink.

She gives an uncomfortable laugh and calls him naughty.

You don't know the half of it, Reg says.

He stares as the waitress retreats.

Yes, Reg says, everything's getting brighter.

It can be hard to get Talia to take her drugs. Talia's always taken medicine reluctantly, hardly even ibuprofen unless she's in bad pain. Now she's on donepezil, a cholinesterase inhibitor to help prevent some sort of breakdown in the chemical messengers in her brain. She also has recently started taking Namenda, which the doctor said is for patients whose problems are getting more severe. Between them, she sometimes gets dizzy. Helping her feels like betraying her. Still, I've tried any number of strategies to persuade her to take her pills. The doctor wrote 'Please take your meds, Talia' on his letterhead and signed it. Invoking the doctor's authority worked for a while. Putting on some Vivaldi softly in the background can help keep things positive, particularly on days when the sunlight fills the kitchen, washing against the wood floors, the oak cabinets. I've learned the hard way that her beloved Beethoven is simply too intense to encourage compliance. Sometimes she seems to come right for a moment, and she understands what she's taking and why. Those spells don't last, though, and I've not been able to find a pattern to predict them.

Once, wholly unable to persuade her, at my wits' end, I tossed the medicine into some apricot yoghurt: the sugar-laden kind for which she'd always had an affinity, a treat she permitted herself only occasionally, disciplined as she has always been, the sort she would never let me purchase for her. I think she saw it as a kind of defeat when she gave in and bought it for herself. She'd taken the spoonful into her mouth and was swallowing when she looked up, a sudden clarity in her eyes, the trace of that old wicked smile tugging her mouth.

Oh, Stephen, she'd said. Really? In the yoghurt? I must be making you desperate.

Then she was gone again, and I was feeding a stranger.

I wonder whether Talia's mind alights on her affair, which took place a few years into our marriage. She was so young, five years my junior, and if I'm honest with myself she had married me out of a kind of convenience. Not that she hasn't loved me all of these years. She has in her way. But we met not long after she'd come out of a relationship with someone she'd known at the conservatory and, in a real way, our marriage was both a reaction to that loss and an attempt to go the other direction, to find someone outside of music, though still in some way in sympathy with craft. I was engrossed in writing my first novel, and she must not have been prepared for the isolation she felt. I certainly hadn't learned yet to balance my obsessive writing against her needs — that came later. Her affair lasted just a few months. That I stumbled on this information a decade and a half after it ended made negotiating the effect of that affair more difficult. It was powerfully new for me, a fresh injury, while for her it was history, feeling long faded to thought. I think sometimes about the long summer of my coming to grips with what she'd done. Funny what you remember. We had a hawk in the yard. Michael was riding his bicycle to piano lessons every morning.

What is a sonata? This is the question Beethoven asked implicitly throughout all of his sonatas, according to Talia's book. I've been reading in her manuscript about Sonata No. 30 in E Major, Op. 109. Over the course of his life Beethoven stretched the sonata form beyond what any listener of, say, Mozart might have expected. But one of the great delights of Op. 109 — the first of his three late sonatas, as they are frequently referred to — is that the first movement is in a very recognisable sonata form. I put the CD on and immediately hear the great contrasts between the two themes, not just harmonically but in style: The first theme is marked by a regular rhythm, while the second is flexible, even impressionistic. But Beethoven plays with the strictness of the form. It is a severely strict form — pared down (the first movement can be played in less than four minutes, as Talia's book notes, one of his shortest sonata movements) — so that part of the pleasure lies with how he has pushed the sonata form not outward but inward, to its essentials, so that he is playing with our expectations by adhering to them — as if joking with us, as if suggesting that we reconsider the importance of formal expectation: *You want the sonata form? Here it is.* And, yet, it isn't.

In her book, Talia argues that Op. 109 confounds our expectations precisely by over-fulfilling them, that he fulfils our expectation for variation to such a degree that we feel just a bit chastised for having the expectation at all: In the third movement, we have not just six variations on a theme, but variations on variations, in what one commentator has called a kind of thematic 'Russian doll'. Again, by meeting our expectations to such a degree, Beethoven overturns them: It is hard without repeated hearings (and perhaps even then) to hear the original theme in some of these variations, since repetition has — like the form — been stretched beyond recognition.

Talia and I met at a party that I didn't want to attend. It was April, and I was finishing graduate school, a master's in English. I had a difficult thesis to complete and, since I'd been given a low-wage teaching assistantship, two sections of freshman English assignments to grade. The papers, nearly fifty of them, sat in a mountainous stack, casting a shadow over the weekend. It was Geoff who persuaded me. Work often came easily to Geoff, and when it didn't he hardly minded. I admired and envied the way he could spend twelve hours in a lab then emerge bouncing, ready for play, an ease in life that made things always, from my perspective, go just right for him, and which I continued to admire and envy for the length of our friendship. I'd spend eight hours at a carrel in the library or on the worn couch in the living room of the cramped, dirty house I shared with three other graduate students on a loud corner of a loud neighbourhood — too many undergraduates, as it turned out — and then could think of nothing I wanted less than to talk to people. I suppose I was an introvert, and in that little has changed.

There is this thing called human company, Geoff said that day, lying full length on the couch. Its legs were uneven, so if he shifted the entire couch moved.

I'd recently returned from the library. My head hurt. I was sitting on the easy chair, my legs resting on what passed as a coffee table — an old, dented trunk that one of my housemates had stumbled on god knows where. Books were piled by my feet on the trunk, more books and papers in a dishevelled pile on the floor.

Haven't heard of it, I said.

So I gather.

Geoff left the room. I heard familiar noises in the kitchen, then he returned with two open beers.

It's Friday night, he said, handing me one.

Technically, the beers belong to Daniel, I said.

Geoff was well aware of this. Daniel, a grad student in history, had found the rental and advertised for roommates, which is how I came to be there. Geoff knew, as well, that this gave Daniel a sense, however false, of ownership of the house.

He won't mind, Geoff said.

Of course not. As I recall one of the rules of the house is 'strict respect for private property.'

And respect it I shall, Geoff said, tilting his nearly

vertical. There are half a dozen others in there, he added after his swallow, and I'll drink all of them to put myself out of my misery if we have to sit here.

So I wound up with Geoff at the party. It wasn't the sort of party I was expecting. What I expected was to walk to a crappy student rental house crowded with people, little room to move, awkward conversation over loud music, bottles of half-finished beer on every surface, potato chips crunching underfoot. Instead, Geoff drove us in the car he'd inherited from his father half an hour to a rather flash neighbourhood. The street was quiet, a half-dozen cars lined up in front of the house. It was one of those houses in vogue in the seventies, with a steeply pitched roof that had a half-timber decorative detail, two storeys, twin gables, diamond-shaped glass. I suppose now I'd find it kitsch, but at the time it seemed massive and impressive. The lawn was neatly trimmed, and the garden seemed professionally managed, though I couldn't tell for certain — maybe everyone in this neighbourhood had time to garden.

I kept to the front path and felt underdressed in the same jeans I'd worn for two days and an old shirt. Geoff as usual was dressed in the perfect balance, his shirt untucked but clean, new and patterned, the sleeves wound halfway up his arms, his hair — still a bit blond back then — longish, but not long. As we approached the house, I could start to hear the murmur of voices. I also heard music. Not the blaring of speakers I was expecting, but the sound of a piano. Classical music, though it would be years before I could recognise the piece or the composer.

When we walked up the steps to the wide front porch, the door stood directly in front of us. To the left and right were windows into front rooms. I stood looking through the left-hand window. A woman sat at a piano, her back to me. I could see only her curly, red hair, her slender, freckled shoulders laid bare in her dress, the movements of her hands when they shifted to either side of her body and, now and again, just barely the side of her face, her eyes closed, the last few minutes of a life before she knew me, wholly unaware that I was watching, fully in the present.

Orville takes up jogging. Or takes it up again. He'd gone through a jogging phase forty years earlier. Back then, in the late seventies, he'd been reading a book by a man famous for starting the jogging fad, Jim Fixx whose runner's legs were on the cover. Orville at the time had been into the particulars, what they now call the gear — the correct running shoes. Fixx became hugely famous on the back of his running books. Then he died at fifty-two of a heart attack while jogging. Turns out that all the cigarettes he'd smoked and pounds he'd gained before he became a runner might have taken their toll. Or maybe it was congenital — Orville can't recall. There are some things you can't outrun.

Still, the fad stuck, and Orville had kept it up for five or six years before other things displaced it. And now, all these years later, he feels strong enough to pick it up. He stretches carefully in the living room, surprised to find he can no longer recall the precise stretches he used to do, but improvises. He takes his time, closes the door behind him, stuffs the key into the potted plant farthest from the door, and takes off down the street. Orville is prepared to make it a short run, but instead he feels exhilarated. He can feel it in his legs and in his chest, but it's not a feeling of exhaustion. He runs past the mailbox three blocks from his house, runs through a small park, up a hill, then on to a neighbourhood jogging path. He passes a couple in their thirties (the man keeps looking at this watch, while the woman talks in gulping breaths), taking in the trees on either side of him — oaks, maples — the trial six weeks in, the first autumn colour coming on. The sweat is streaming down his face, slipping beneath his sunglasses — he needs to get a headband or something — but he wipes it away and keeps going. A younger man passes him, probably about forty, and as he does so the man nods his head in greeting. It is so surprising that Orville has to stop, look back at the man running down the path as he adjusts his earphones, then disappears around the lake. The feeling of being acknowledged. You can start to feel prematurely like a ghost when you get into your seventies — Orville knows a man in his late seventies who wears a red beret almost everywhere, calling it his 'visibility cloak'. Orville has spent so long by now feeling invisible that to be seen by someone so young has to be absorbed. Strange to be returned by a glance to flesh and blood.

No matter how often I listen to Sonata 30, no matter how hard I try to attend to the structure that Talia lays out with such care in her book, I can only maintain it for brief moments. I lose track of the structure because this piece is very much about feelings. I can nearly hear what the 'speaker' of this first movement is saying, just as via intonation and gesture it is possible to nearly translate the speech of someone speaking a foreign language. But there is also the delicacy and simplicity of its statement — of emotions of great complexity: sadness but not hopelessness. It is perhaps best expressed as longing. The second movement will not leave me to linger in such longing — there is a defiance in its near-angry sentiments. But as with all anger and defiance, it gives way, at the end, to a kind of compromise, a resolution coloured by oppositions. It is the kind of resolution that can exist only after the initial peace has been disturbed; that is, it concludes, finally, with the not-quite-peaceful peace of someone who has gone through an emotional wringer — the peace, I guess, of adulthood, not childhood.

The temperature has dropped and I think about lighting the fire. Anna brought back Talia just as it started to rain and took Talia to her room for a nap. I offered Anna a cup of coffee as a matter of course, but she declined as I knew she would and left. She remains so kind to Talia, though until Talia's illness and Michael's death we had hardly seen her for some time. I was hardly in a position to be as much help to her when Geoff died at the end of last year, when Anna carried her own grief.

I sit on the couch, looking at the dark fireplace. The brick facade, the gold of the metal curtain, they are dated now, but so familiar to me that it doesn't matter. I work to gather some energy, to find the psychological alchemy necessary to transform desire into motivation. It will require hefting some wood from the pile in the side yard. There was a time when I used to stack a couple of cords of wood in a single afternoon. Talia liked this about me, when we were early in our marriage. I'm not fat now, but I'm more padded than I was then, and without a regular caregiver for Talia, I've had to cut back on my visits to the gym, which I started some years ago at the suggestion of my doctor. I can feel the difference when I lift the wood. I was wiry and stronger than I realised when I was younger. During graduate school, I worked part-time for a moving company to supplement the paltry teaching assistant stipend during the year and worked full-time for them over the summers. The summer we started to see each other, I worked eight hours a day moving boxes, pushing pianos onto the truck, lifting bed frames, oak dressers, coffee tables, couches. It was exhausting, the days hot. I can't pretend that I didn't enjoy Talia's reaction to my body, particularly toward summer's end, when I was as ripped as I'd ever been or would ever be and we had moved into an apartment together (one advantage of working for a moving company was a free truck and some help from one of my workmates). She'd come up behind me when I'd gotten out of the shower (she wouldn't touch me when I came home covered in grime and dried sweat — *Toss those clothes directly into the basket*, she'd say). She'd run her hands over my chest. *Grade A beef*, she'd joke.

She loved that our house had this fireplace. For a while we ran through two cords a year. I'd stack it in the woodshed I'd built on the side of the house, nothing fancy — basically a lean-to. Michael loved the fire, too. The metal curtain across it got quite hot, and he burned his finger when he was three after ignoring our instructions to stay back. He cried for an hour. But that was the only incident, and it didn't put him off. Sometimes, we roasted marshmallows on it, small plates on the stone tiles in front. When he was five, Michael insisted on 'helping' me to build the fire. He would crumple newspaper and hand it to me to place on the grate. He helped me to gather sticks from the yard and, when he was a bit older, helped me to prune the many trees we have in our yard, break them up, and drag them into the garage, where we let them dry all summer in boxes, so that we had plenty of kindling in the winter. We got the newspaper on Sundays, and Talia kept stacks of unread sections that interested her and which she'd hoped to return to when she had more time, stacks that accumulated on the bottom of her bookshelf. When they got tall enough, I'd take the bottom third and pile it in the garage, by the kindling. It was a game we played. Too busy to read through it all, she couldn't get herself to toss out all the book reviews, art stories and editorial sections that she still hoped to read, so she would pretend not to notice that

I'd regularly remove the oldest ones. I think she was relieved not to have to read them. At some point, we started to use the fire less often, until we were burning far less than a cord each winter. Eventually, too, I gave up on stacking it, small as the annual batch is. The delivery men stack it for me now in the woodshed. It takes two of them about twenty minutes, and their stacks, I have to admit, are sturdier, more stable than mine, practised. I stand to look out of the living-room window at the roof of the woodshed. It's raining lightly. I take my jacket off the peg at the kitchen door and go out to the shed, bring back an armload of wood, the rich smell of the pine in my face. I put it in a basket by the fireplace then go back out to the garage to get some old newspaper and some kindling. As I build the fire, I try to focus only on the actions I'm taking, actions so familiar that I could be taking them anytime in the past three decades.

Soon I have it going. I kneel there, in front of the fire — until my knees ache and I have to straighten them, move to the couch — and think about Michael's last visit. The files piled on the dining room table. Michael helping Talia to sort through her notes, looking at her manuscript on the laptop, offering suggestions, playing bits on the piano and disagreeing with her even as she smiled at him. Then the abrupt departure, two days earlier than planned. The slam of the door, the sight of his rental car turning the corner. The long silence since.

And Orville? It's hard to know what to make of him, getting younger and stronger. Stories aren't about growing younger and stronger, though, are they? Narrative is messy business, entropy the rule in this particular universe, the only one we know. Bad things happen to all of us in time, and he's moving forward through time like the rest of us, not backward, even if his body seems to be. Moving forward inevitably draws us into instability. Best not to make the mistake of thinking that reversing decline means moving to a greater simplicity, to anything like ease. If I can take my anger out on someone, why not poor Orville, with his skin smoothing out, his greater grasp of colour and line, his increasingly chiselled frame, his libido alight? *Another of your redemptions in progress,* Talia would say, if she were still Talia. But I suppose I wouldn't be writing it then.

The crackling, the scent of the smoke, and the heat draw Talia from her room to the couch. It's been years since a marshmallow has crossed our threshold — since Michael was a boy — but I suddenly miss it powerfully. I imagine ripping open the packet, putting a marshmallow on one of the sticks in the kindling pile, browning it carefully (as Talia used to do) or letting it catch fire (as Michael preferred to do) and tasting the caramelised burnt flavor along with the underlying sugar, its heat sometimes scorching my tongue, the goo getting on hands (*Go straight to the sink and wash them, Michael — no, don't touch anything*). I can't drive to the store and leave Talia here, though, and it seems too much to take her through the rain and drag her through the aisles for what will no doubt be a treat that pales beside its memory. So I sit by Talia and stare with her into the fire, feel the intensity of its heat on my face as it both warms the room and draws the air from it, yesterday's news, all the words that once mattered, turned to ash and the smoke that spreads into the air above the house then disappears.

TWO

Michael saw it first. I might not have believed him if he hadn't held out his binoculars. I'd been in the front yard, clipping bushes. Mid-July and I kept thinking to go inside and get a hat. That would have entailed walking through the kitchen, where Talia was writing. Sooner or later, I'd have to interact with her, but I wasn't interested in dealing with that at the moment. Instead, I kept lifting my hand to my brow, wiping sweat with the dirty gardening glove. Michael came running from around the house, insisting that I come to the backyard to look at the hawk.

It's probably not a hawk, I said.

I followed, though. Michael handed over the binoculars and pointed toward the tree. Without the binoculars, I couldn't see a thing in the tree. But when I lifted them to my eyes and spent a few moments searching around, I found the nest. A hawk alright, perched high and deep in the pine. I'd never seen one up close, if this was considered close, and had never known one to perch in the yard or, for that matter, in the neighbourhood.

You're right, I said. Babies, too.

Let me see.

He took back the binoculars. I looked at my son. Twelve years old and I could see in his face the hint of what he might look like at sixteen or eighteen. He still had some freckles across his nose. His hair was bushy and curly, darker than mine. He needed a haircut, but at twelve he still didn't care about that; it was an effort to persuade him to take a shower or comb his hair at all. He wore a pair of khaki shorts and a yellow local music festival T-shirt that he'd picked up earlier in the summer. It was his favourite T-shirt, and the words and the large notes (rising like balloons) on the front were already fading from repeated use and washing. He was growing so fast, though, that the shirt wouldn't last him a year anyway. He was already five feet, up two inches in the past year. I had topped out at 5 feet, 11 inches. Part of me hoped my son would exceed that, part of me hoped he wouldn't.

Michael asked what the hawks were doing here. I admitted I didn't know. Michael had been a very smart kid from go, and I'd long gotten used to admitting my ignorance on any number of topics. I knew nothing about their nesting patterns, their habits. Had something changed in the landscape that had pushed them into suburbs (which is what our little town was essentially becoming as Boulder pushed north)? Was it the way development was encroaching into the foothills? Or was there something about the houses here the hawk found particularly attractive? I thought about kittens and the occasional chicken that some neighbours were keeping in their yards, the mice that made their way into the attic.

Michael said, I wonder if we can get it to come down closer.

I was wary. Among the many other things I didn't know about hawks was how they reacted to people. They were large birds, powerful ones, predators. Not that I imagined one could pick up and carry off a twelve year old — this hawk, in fact, seemed on the smaller side — but who knew what damage it might be able to do if it felt threatened.

How were you planning to 'get it' to come down?

I don't know. Put some food out for it, I guess.

Give it some space, I said. Let's find out a bit more first. Also, animals tend to be a bit short-tempered if you come near their young.

Michael nodded and turned back to his binoculars. Don't worry, Dad, he said. I'm not going to throw rocks at it or anything.

That's mighty reassuring.

I looked up past the tree. The sun was overhead. It must have been thirty-five degrees. I wiped sweat from my brow for the hundredth time.

Why don't you go in and get something to eat? I said.

I will in a minute, Dad.

I could have used some lunch myself. I was thirsty, too, and imagined a tall glass of cranberry juice and seltzer on ice. But the kitchen was dangerous territory. I walked back around to the front yard and picked up the clippers.

The hawk became a fixture of the summer. Every morning, before breakfast, Michael took his binoculars to the backyard, searched for the hawk, afraid it was gone, found it or its two babies in the nest, came back inside already sweaty.

Talia was home, writing. She didn't have to start teaching again until the last week of August. I was nearly always home working on a book as well. We were constantly walking past one another. Michael was spending the summer in intensive training, piano lessons every day and several hours of practice after that, with Talia listening, if sometimes only with one ear.

Soon, we established a pattern. After breakfast, Michael biked to his lesson, about three miles away. While he was gone, Talia and I largely avoided each other by retreating to our separate corners to work, she in the kitchen — she liked the light afforded by the many windows — and I to the study, darker, what she'd called in more affectionate times 'the cave'. She'd insisted years before that I get the study, since she had an office on campus. I'd protested weakly, but I was happy to have it.

It was in some ways easier when Michael was home. We could both speak naturally to him, and the various ways he occupied our attention made our own silences less oppressive. I hoped they were less obvious to Michael. I was glad about the hawk, too. It kept a portion of his attention focused outward. It gave him something to think about besides piano, and an excuse to be outside.

One morning, he stopped at the library on the way home from his lesson to get a few books on hawks. He looked through them for a few minutes at lunch and after dinner. In between, he practised. He took one of the books outside and looked at pictures, then with his binoculars looked back at the bird. I think it might be a sharp-shinned hawk, he said.

This is what I remember about that month in summer: Afternoons writing in my study, the sound of the air conditioner straining to keep the house to twenty-two degrees, a box fan on a chair by my desk, blowing papers that I had to hold down with books, a plate. Talia, miles away down the hall in the kitchen, tapping away on her keyboard on the old Macintosh she lugged on and off the kitchen table, the sound of her chair scraping the linoleum, the rushing of the kitchen tap and the clattering of the coffee pot. The aroma of the brewing coffee working its way through the air, a scent soon associated with the sound of the piano, both of them filling the house, Michael playing a piece half-way through, then again and again, day after day, repetition and return.

Talia suggested we contact the state wildlife department to be sure we had nothing to worry about with a hawk in our yard, and a few hours later a state pick-up truck pulled up. A young man in blue jeans and a Parks and Wildlife shirt, thin with dark hair that reached over his ears and slipped down his neck, identified himself as biologist. He was excited to see the hawk. We showed him around back, where he used his own binoculars to investigate.

Cooper's hawk, he said. But — turning to Michael — you were close: it looks a lot like the sharp-shinned. He handed his binoculars to Michael. See the way her crown — the top of her head — is a bit darker than the rest, like she's wearing a beret?

The biologist's name was Aaron. He actually wasn't as young as I'd thought initially — he was thirty-two, he said, had gotten his master's a few years earlier and stayed in the area. He said he supposed he could remove the bird if it bothered us. Some people don't like that they eat other birds at their feeders. We said we were happy to have the hawk and had no bird feeders. Aaron was glad to hear it, said that it was good to let the hawk be for now, at least until the chicks leave the nest.

We invited him in for a cup of coffee, and he talked about hawks. It turns out the Cooper's hawk was starting to be seen in towns like ours a few miles outside urban centres, but also increasingly in more populated suburbs.

They like eating birds best, Aaron said — pigeons and, if they can find them, doves. Maybe you've heard them called chickenhawks. But they'll also eat mice or squirrels, chipmunks, hares. He explained that unlike, say, falcons, the hawks don't kill their prey with a quick bite. Instead, they hold it away from their bodies until it dies or sometimes fly it to a nearby lake or pond, holding it beneath the surface until it drowns.

Michael said he'd seen the hawk spread its wings once and it was huge.

Actually, Aaron said, Cooper's are a bit small for hawks. When Michael looked disappointed, Aaron added, but still impressive. You've definitely got a female. The males are pretty small and passive. They're afraid of the women because the female Cooper's hawk likes to eat smaller birds. (At this, Michael raised his eyebrows in interest.) So the males build the nests and then keep their distance, even giving little bows after mating, and otherwise taking care around the females. They only come close if they're called. No sense in getting their heads bitten off. He took a sip of coffee, looked at Talia, then gave me a wink.

Michael was at his morning lesson. I'd come into the kitchen to get a cup of coffee. Talia had set up her usual spot in the kitchen, hefting the Mac onto the table, a pile of folders beside her.

We have to talk about this, she said.

It was the first time she had brought up the subject. I was starting to wonder if either of us ever would. I'd tried to talk about it early on, but it had been a disaster. When she spoke, I had the milk in my hand, the door of the fridge propped on my arm. I bought time by closing the door with my foot, pouring the milk into the coffee.

I said, you're acting as though I'm the one with the problem.

Talia had tied her hair back tightly but the strength

of her tight curls and the mass of her hair resisted, already loosening against the band. She was getting mid-morning sunlight, and for the first time it seemed to me that her face was in fact older. I had probably spent years looking at her but not really seeing her. She wore a black T-shirt, a pair of shorts, bare feet, painted toenails.

Nothing happens in a vacuum, she said.

I see. So it's my fault that you slept with someone else.

It was a long time ago. I'm sorry you've found out now. I realise that makes it fresh for you.

But I should get over it.

Well, yes. I realise that's harsh . . .

Oh, you realise that's harsh, how enlightened of you.

I realise that's harsh, that it's new for you, but it's history. It's not happening. I'm not sure what you'd have me do. I've apologised.

And suggested, just now, that I'm responsible.

Look, obviously I'm responsible. What I'm saying is that it didn't come out of nowhere.

Talia rubbed her eyes. She didn't just look older; she looked tired. For the past few weeks, I'd been sleeping in the living room. I tried to get up and clean up the couch before Michael woke up. Once or twice he'd caught me there, and I'd explained that my back was bothering me, that the couch was easier on it than our old mattress. I don't know if he believed me. I had no idea how Talia was sleeping, but maybe this was bothering her more than she let on.

I said, What was I doing, exactly, that led you to find a lover so early in our marriage? What was my great failure as a husband? Was I beating you? Keeping you in a closet?

This is why I've put off talking about this. You can't talk like an adult.

Like an adult? You mean without any emotion at all? Like I'm talking about someone else?

Yes, good idea. Talk about it as though it were someone else.

There was someone else. That's the whole goddamn problem. You're such a machine, sometimes.

Okay, fuck you, Stephen. Is that better? Human enough?

It's a fairly good imitation.

You *wanted* a machine. I wasn't one. That was the problem.

I'm to blame again.

God, you're such a fucking child. I've said I'm responsible. But it wasn't *just* me. There was our relationship. Can't you admit that?

Exactly. A relationship. Barely off the ground.

Be quiet, Talia said. She put her fingers to her lips. From outside, the rattle of Michael's bike. I could hear him humming a tune. I took my coffee, too cold now, and walked back to the office. Hey, you, I heard Talia say when the screen door closed. How'd it go?

For a week, I mulled over what Talia had said. Was I in some measure responsible? Yes, a lot of time had passed since she had that affair, nearly fifteen years. I'd just found out — she had let it slip during an argument, and I think she was surprised at how it hurt me. The fact of it was old. A lot had happened since then. I thought back to those early days in our marriage. I was writing my first book. In fact, I was spending a lot of time not writing it. I was spending time thinking about it, writing (using an electric typewriter), throwing pages away, staring out of the window, trying to substitute reading and research for the actual work, driving to and from the university library. I was having a hard time, and it seemed to me then that it might never get written, much less published. This would mean, I thought at the time, that I had completely failed before I'd even gotten started. I was teaching a single adjunct course in English to supplement Talia's salary. It wasn't much. We were doing okay, but I felt the pressure of not contributing to the household, that sense of failure as a husband, not just as a writer. Weekly phone conversations with my mother didn't help. *So when do you think you'll be done? So Talia's paying the mortgage?*

Stop listening to your mother, Talia said. I'm fine with it. This isn't 1958.

I said, you're right. Every morning, I went into the study, at first with hope, then later with dread, a sick feeling of waste, of time passing. How long could I go on before it made more sense to give up, to find something full-time? The more supportive Talia became, the more I felt the burden of that support. It became a set of weights on my ankles and wrists. She said she was happy for me to take the time to get this one written, that she wasn't doing any work she wouldn't do anyway — we both came into the marriage knowing we were two people with professional ambitions and aspirations. But in the end I resented her for all of it, for supporting me financially, for her optimism and belief in me. She left the house early, went to the university gym, then to her office, her teaching, her writing. She left me the house, the space I said I needed. Then she came home in the late afternoon, at four or so. She was upbeat, asked me how things went, told me it would be fine. She was so young. When I think about it, she seems in memory somehow fresh, naive. I took it out on her. I replied in grunts, short phrases. I asked why she hadn't stopped for milk. I said did she realise I was working, too. I asked if it was too much for her to make her side of the bed. For the first year or so of our marriage, we used to sit on the couch in the evenings, each with a book, and read passages to each other that we thought were insightful or funny or ridiculously stupid. On Sunday mornings, we'd drive one another into fits of righteous indignation by reading aloud passages from political articles, the latest outrage. I stopped reading things to her because sharing wasn't possible if we weren't equals. She was carrying me. She eventually stopped reading passages aloud to me because I made clear, in expression or gesture if not in words, that she was interrupting me. When I couldn't blame her for something, I would just slam the silverware drawer or the fridge or the glass shower door. I closed too many doors just a little too hard, too often. We were practically newlyweds. I closed too many doors.

Michael started coming home later from his lesson. The first time, instead of 11.30, he showed up at noon. He said he'd stopped at the library. Then it was 12.30, then 1.30. We tried to give him space; he was twelve years old. One day he didn't come home all afternoon. Even Talia, ever composed, looked panicked by 4 pm. I called his piano teacher, who said he'd left at the usual time, quarter after eleven. No, he hadn't said he was going anywhere. No, he didn't seem different or distracted, just the usual Michael.

I scoured the neighbourhood. I drove the route from the teacher's house to the library, stopped in — the librarian didn't remember seeing him. Talia contacted the police, who said they would send out a patrol. But twelve-year-old kids sometimes go off on their own. Call if he's not back by dark.

Michael showed up just before six, smelling of sweat. He dropped his bike on the porch and walked in, as though all were normal. I was not a parent who yelled, but I found myself raising my voice.

What were you thinking?

I was at the library.

Michael, do you think I wouldn't have checked that by now?

You must have missed me.

Nobody remembers you being there.

Well, I was.

And then what?

I don't know.

You can't just disappear like that.

Michael looked away. We were sitting at the kitchen table, and Michael looked through the glass sliding doors, as though hoping the hawk would swoop down to give us something else to talk about.

Michael, you can't vanish all day. What's going on?

Nothing. I was just riding my bike, things like that.

You haven't practised all day.

Michael shrugged. I looked at Talia, who had let me lead the way on this. She shook her head. Meaning, let him be for now.

We'd been too upset between phone calls and searches to think about dinner. We ordered pizza, which seemed more like reward than punishment, ate in near silence. Then Michael picked up on the practice he should have had hours before, Talia watching him from the couch.

Geoff and Anna sat with us on the patio. I had the barbecue going, the lid closed, heating up. Late summer, this had become a weekly ritual. They would come over twice a week, once for a meal Talia cooked inside, once for burgers or steaks or chicken or sausages that I did on the grill; sometimes I improvised something fancier. They were renovating their kitchen, and we offered them these dinners as a respite from the logistical work of cooking in the make-shift kitchen they'd fashioned in a corner of the living room — a microwave, toaster oven, mini-fridge. Ostensibly, that is why we invited them. In truth, it was simply good to have someone else in the house, a way to deflect, even a way for Talia and me to have indirect conversation. They were our good friends, but even in front of them we had to be on somewhat better behaviour with one another.

I left the patio table to put the burgers on the grill. Michael's piano playing was audible but at a low level — nearly a background static. When Geoff slid open the kitchen door to go in, the music blossomed into the backyard before the door closing muffled it. It happened again a moment later as Talia and Anna went inside. Then again when Geoff came back out, bringing two fresh beers. At least I knew Michael was there.

Geoff pulled on his beer. He looked good. He still had his athletic build — he played a lot of tennis in the summer. He'd recently cut his hair very short, though, which made it clear that his head had a kind of pumpkin shape. I hadn't decided whether to tell him or let him keep his illusions.

He said, Michael's sounding really great.

He works at it all the time, I said.

He nodded, turned toward the large pine and shaded his eyes.

How's the hawk?

It appears now and again, I said. It hasn't lost its novelty. Michael's still out there every morning looking for it. I can get you Michael's binoculars if you're interested.

Maybe later, he said.

I'd seen the hawk up close just two days earlier. Talia had gone out on an errand, a haircut appointment (she came back with her hair a lot shorter, something spritely, which made her seem young again). Michael was still at his lesson. Alone in the house, I walked through all of the rooms, found myself in the kitchen. Her Mac was on the table, along with her usual profusion of folders. I sat at the other end of the table, drinking coffee, enjoying toast. It was nice not to have to fit a plate on my crowded desk. Eating in my own kitchen, I felt like a prisoner on furlough.

I was reading a newspaper as I ate, but I sensed a movement out of the corner of my eye, through the glass doors. The hawk had landed on the patio table, a black wrought-iron piece we'd picked up at a used furniture store years before and which had held up well. I'd thought, then, about the way objects stay with us, persist through time, and that they are the only way we can be sure those times actually happened. I had recently come to understand that was the function of a souvenir, no matter how cheap or kitschy — the snow globes, key chains. Even the chipped mug with my old college's name on it, the one I kept pens in on my desk, had become a kind of rock in the stream of time, something to prove that memories were not wholly inventions. Perched on the table, the hawk looked at me, then looked away, then back, as though trying to make a decision. It seemed the symbol of all that was transitory and unlikely. We stared at each other for several minutes. The glass seemed a flimsy separation between its world and mine. Then it spread its wings. The gesture was so sudden, the wingspan so large up close, I involuntarily jerked back, spilled the coffee, the liquid stretching down the table toward Talia's computer. I threw some napkins down before it did damage, the computer safe, only a dark spot at the edge of a folder on the bottom of the pile, something I hoped Talia wouldn't notice. Then the hawk was gone.

I told this to Geoff. Then I said, But now it's hard to believe it happened that way.

He said, when you remember something it's not even like you're hacking a new path through the jungle. It's not even the same jungle.

Without realising I was going to do it, I said, Talia had an affair.

Geoff's beer bottle was poised in the air. He lowered his arm, took a sharp breath.

She told you that?

She admitted it, I said. We were arguing, and it came out.

He looked at me closely, waiting for me to continue.

I said, Someone named Rob.

Rob?

She didn't want to say at first who but I pressed her. Bullied her, I guess. That's all she would give me. She told me who he was in general terms, admitted it was a musician she'd met. Someone involved in one of the concerts or something she did. It was nearly fifteen years ago. She refused to give me more details.

Did you know him?

No. She says we never met.

I don't know what to say.

What's to say? It happened. It didn't go on for long, a few months. Like I said, it happened years ago. Long over. It's just new for me. I haven't had those years to absorb it.

Jesus.

Yeah.

Geoff took a swallow of his beer, looked away, back out into the yard. He rubbed his face. It was nearly 6.30, the sun still visible, still casting warm light onto the patio, now starting its descent, moving toward the tops of the pines. The women were still inside, doing who knows what. Behind the faint sounds of the piano, I could hear the murmuring of the creek at the base of the hill. The late sunlight caught Geoff's face as he looked back into the yard. In the light, his hair was not just shorter but thinner, his face haggard. Why was everyone looking so tired? It occurred to me, then, that maybe he and Anna were going through a patch. It was a sudden feeling. I thought about their kitchen renovations, the way improving one thing can make us feel like we're improving another.

He turned back to me. Does Michael . . .

Of course not, I said. I mean, I'm sure he senses something, but we're trying to keep things normal. Or whatever passes for normal. He catches me sleeping on the couch sometimes.

I guess I sensed some tension, Geoff said. But this . . .

It's good to have you guys around.

So, Geoff said carefully, where does that leave the two of you?

We're in a holding pattern, I said.

I thought to myself, That's exactly right. We're just trying to make it through the summer. Just waiting for some sign of a change of season. We're perched, poised, alert.

I looked around the table. We'd all squeezed around it on the patio, with the steaks, the salad, the corn that Anna and Geoff had contributed heated in foil on the grill. Michael came out to join us only long enough to shove down his food, look around the for the birds — not in evidence — then go back inside. No piano music ensued, and I wondered what Michael was doing. I understood it would be boring to sit with us at the table. I wished sometimes that we'd given him a sibling. Michael had few friends. His best friend, Lewis — also a musician, the viola — was away a lot that summer with his parents.

Anna and Geoff didn't have children. They'd tried for years and were, I knew, discussing whether to adopt or to abandon the project. Talia was talking about Michael's repertoire, about his progress. One of her favourite subjects. She spoke animatedly, hands gesturing — taking on the fingering of the piano as she described one of the pieces — her face flushed. She spoke mainly to Anna, with occasional glances to Geoff. I wondered whether all this talk about Michael was rude, was painful to Anna. She wanted to adopt children less, I knew, than Geoff did. Geoff had indicated on a few occasions that this was a source of tension between them. Not just their failure to have children but their different responses to that failure, Anna's a deep regret that only biology could repair and Geoff's a sense that the hole could be filled more easily, his refusal to acknowledge Anna's very different sense of things. This was the other side to Geoff's ease in the world, the ease I'd always admired and in no small way envied. That ease required Geoff's full attention, required him to remain nimble, unburdened. Geoff was a generous friend, but his generosity was delimited by its connection to his own well-being. He'd always made things easier for me so that they would be easier for himself. Geoff was in that respect, though deeply intellectual, someone who preferred to skim the social surface. Anna had her hair, light brown, tied in a pony tail, wore a sleeveless top, a skirt that she'd let fold up to expose her right knee, crossed over her left. Her eyes were set too close together, always giving her face a kind of concerned look. It came across not as irritation or worry but as though she were in some way anxious for you, that your feelings were foremost in her mind. As though aware I was watching her, she flipped the cloth across to cover her knee. The sense I had earlier that Talia was growing older came back to me. Her hair was still red, a few strands of silver in the light. The new haircut gave her an energetic look. It was the shape of her face, the skin bunching a bit under her chin, the texture of the skin itself. Geoff, too. He was still in great shape, no sign of belly through his polo as he sat in the chair — all that tennis. He seemed simply to be shifting into a new phase, took up more space. No, it wasn't space. It was mass, density. There was a heaviness about him that distinguished who he was now from the ease with which he'd glided through life when we'd been in school. He displaced more of the world in a way that had nothing to do with his weight or height. The way Geoff rubbed his hand across his face, sat back in his chair watching Talia speak, attentive but not really to her words. I realised suddenly that Geoff was probably evaluating her, just as I was doing, that we were both engaged in this moment in a way that was observational rather than participatory. I was finishing my third beer, could feel the alcohol. Suddenly, as a kind of flash, I found myself looking at all three of them as if they were near-strangers. For a moment, it was as though all of the earlier incarnations of these people — the twenty years we'd been friends — had been cut away, so that I saw them for who they really were at the moment, distinct from my preconceptions and feelings about them, no longer the palimpsests of their many selves. It felt as though I were looking from childhood at the people who would populate my future. Three middle-aged people sitting at a table. Who were these people? How did I get here?

Now Talia was describing the fight. Earlier in the week, the two baby hawks — well, not babies anymore — scuffled on the garage roof. I'd heard the noise, ran out to find them knocking each other around. It seemed like a real fight, but who could tell. I didn't see any blood. Maybe it was just play, two brothers getting into a scrap. Talia came out of the kitchen with my camera, spoke normally as if there were no problem between us, said we should be documenting all of this. I pointed the lens at the two hawks, snapped as many photos as I could as they seemed to peck at each other, tumble across the roof, before one of them fell off and launched into the air.

Instead of writing, I'd spent that day taking photographs. I took shots of the hawks when they appeared, took photos of Michael on his bike riding down the street, then down the driveway. Photos of Michael at the piano, of Talia at the Mac at the kitchen table, of the two of them — mother and son — at the piano bench. I took photos almost desperately, I suppose, as though there were something I didn't want to miss or to forget, a feeling I knew I had but could not articulate. I finished the roll that day, took it to the drugstore to get developed.

That was five days earlier and the prints came back that morning. I hadn't told Talia. I looked at the three of them, Talia describing the hawks. Anna leaning forward in her chair on one side, chin on her hand, a light fist. Geoff on the other side leaning forward, participating now, his arm loosely around Talia's chair, laughing at the way she described the scene, as though she were describing two people who were acting wholly inappropriately at an important social event. Talia knew her own reputation for propriety, and, when she was relaxed, she could exaggerate it for humour, making herself, rather than what she described, the true source of amusement. I had looked through the prints. Many of them were blurry, poorly lit — I'd never been a great photographer. A few good ones, though. One of Talia and Michael at the piano, a light moment I'd witnessed and managed to catch, Michael's hands at the keyboard, his face an exaggerated mask of intensity and portension, Talia's head tilted back in laughter. The two young hawks on the roof, just at the edge, at one another's throats.

The next time, Michael didn't show up for dinner.

Talia and I enlisted the help of Geoff and Anna, who both took time from work to drive around looking for him. The police agreed again to send out a patrol car.

I tried the library several times over several hours. Though I knew Michael wouldn't be there, each time I walked into the cool dark of the building, looked at each table, made a pass through every stack. I drove around town before it occurred to me that I needed to think like my son. Or, if I couldn't think like him, I had to see the world the way Michael saw it. I returned home for my bicycle. I hadn't ridden the bike in years, so I had to spend what felt like precious time pumping up the tires, feeling ridiculous, wondering if this was simply stupid, hoping Talia — cruising around town separately in the Subaru — wouldn't surprise me and show this for the waste of time it might be. I tried to remember the last time I rode it, an old mountain bike I'd bought before Michael was born. The last time must have been when Michael was eight. Talia and I still felt uncomfortable then having Michael riding alone. I'd accompanied Michael to his friends' houses — mainly Lewis's house. The bike was dusty, but with the tires pumped, it seemed serviceable. I climbed on and set off in the direction of town, about fifteen minutes down the hill.

Strange to be trying to find Michael. He was in a new phase now, one I recognised, the start of a gradual widening of distance. It made me realise I missed the days when he couldn't wait to see us when he was gone and we always knew where he was. It gave me regret, too, in realising how quickly that time went. I remember appreciating the couple of weekend hours when he was younger and went to Sunday school, the relief from parenting, but now that appreciation, that relief, feels foolish and self-centred. Not that he was in Sunday school long, just two years, the time it took Talia to decide she did not need to repeat her own upbringing. Though a lapsed Catholic, she initially took it as a matter of course that Michael would get some sort of religious education. So critically acute about most things, it was one of the few times I've seen her mindlessly follow a script, at least until she abruptly pulled Michael from class. She claimed then that it was to free up his time — he spent so much of it practising the piano that it seemed reasonable enough. But the true reason, I think, was the death of her father. Her father had been a staunch Catholic — he was not initially pleased, to put it mildly, that she'd married someone outside the fold, though he was unfailingly polite to me and, I think, came around to me as a person. Her mother had died a few years before. Her father was the one person I'd ever see her work so hard to please, whose judgements seemed to affect her. From the outside, it was hard to fathom since he was a fairly unassuming person, often quiet, not given to soap-box lectures. With his slim build — he grew thinner, not thicker in old age — he never struck me as an imposing presence. But fathers are fathers, I suppose. When he died, I think she was finally free to be herself, which is to say someone who thinks acutely and critically, with enough distance that no ideology stood a chance, however inviting its claims.

Not sure exactly where I was headed, I rode down Apple Valley Road, caught occasional glimmers of the creek through the trees. I slowed, looked for a passage through them. Eventually, about a mile along, I found a small trail, a path tamped down through use, the grass flattened and worn. It was the type to attract boys on bikes.

The trail was dry, the grass area brown from drought before the path through the trees. There were tracks through the dirt, bikes and feet. I followed it along as it became flat, covered with pine needles. I could see the creek. The path grew more difficult then, trees closer together, so I dismounted, walked the bike. Then I spotted Michael. Nearly 7 pm, the light starting to fade. It would be gone in an hour. Michael sat by the creek, his bike propped on a tree about twenty feet behind him. He sat on a rock, hugging his knees, staring into the water. Then he reached down, picked up a stone, tossed it in. Michael shouldn't be here, past dinner, shouldn't be hiding in the woods, his parents panicked. Still, I felt suddenly like an interloper, a trespasser into my son's interior life, as though I'd read Michael's journal.

Michael, absorbed in whatever he was thinking, sitting beside the murmuring water, seemed not to have heard me. After a few minutes, I walked my bike back up the trail. I headed off to the right, propped the bike near a tree and waited. Half an hour later, Michael came through, walking his bike back to the road, took off in the direction of home. I couldn't tell if he'd been crying, wondered whether Michael had been here all day, how hungry he might be. I waited until Michael was on the road, then set out, followed my son home. Hoping he didn't know I was there, I kept well behind, losing Michael around bends, spotting him, then losing him again, trying to gauge a safe distance, wondering whether that more or less summarised family life that summer, whether the phrase 'family life' amounts in some important sense to a contradiction, an oxymoron.

I beat my brain for some remnant of Rob, some crumb of conversation, a time when she'd mentioned him. I looked through photographs of Talia's concerts, using a magnifying glass to examine the faces of the musicians in the background. I needed to know who he was, needed to pin the elusive butterfly of his face to the board of the present so that I could put this whole thing into the objective perspective it required. It happened nearly a decade and a half earlier and I couldn't think who to ask, much less how to ask a friend or colleague of hers from those days, without giving away the story, without raising suspicions. She claimed it was a musician, but how could I know for sure? It made sense: I could only imagine it must have been someone she spent time with on those occasions she was not at home, and on those occasions she was nearly always involved in music — rehearsals, concerts, after-parties, some of which I did not attend.

What had those days been like, exactly? I went to most of her concerts; she didn't expect me to go to everything, just as I didn't expect her to always attend the readings I occasionally gave then. It was a beautiful thing to watch her play. She had several dresses that she wore only on those occasions. She was never the type to stand at her closet, hands on her hips, lost, trying on multiple sets of clothes, leaving them scattered on the bed. She simply opened the door and extracted a dress, and once she had taken a dress from the closet, she never asked for my opinion. She knew what she wanted, knew how she wanted to look, and that poise with which she carried herself in private continued without interruption as she walked across the stage, as she sat at the keyboard. That she had passion I knew from the privacy of our moments, but it was a passion she kept under tight rein, the sort she seemed nearly to regret once it passed. The woman whose mouth had been pressing on mine, legs wrapped around my own, appetite voracious — her existence was always limited, a woman replaced quickly when my eyes were closed, when I left for the bathroom. Her feelings, her desire, were like a challenging conversation she needed at times to cut off. I wondered whether her own limitations as a pianist, as an artist, were connected to her need to control those passions. The academy made more sense for her: a life requiring more discipline than desire, or at least permitting a much more flexible mix of such ingredients. How deeply, I wondered, did a pianist have to dig to connect with a Beethoven sonata? Technical skill was one thing, but those are means, aren't they? Just the tools? What if there was a point beyond which she could not go, could not let go? All of those talented pianists who never quite made it. Some necessary mix of technical prowess, discipline, desire, but also feeling — not just feeling but the willingness to engage with those feelings, to let them be what they are. Is that what talent is?

But she did engage those passions, didn't she? At least for a while. With someone called Rob. This invisible man, this blank face. Someone who gave her license to let go of that poise with which she walked carefully through the world. I tried to imagine it. Where did they go, these two lovers? How long did each tryst endure? Was it an hour, an entire day? What sort of person was she with him, and did the release from herself that he clearly provided extend to how she acted with him in their less intimate moments, the moments when they were among others, the moments when they walked to a hotel or his home or wherever it was they went to be together alone? Did she giggle like the girl she rarely permitted herself to be with me? Did she allow him to mock her playfully?

I tried to imagine what he looked like, what it was

about his manner that gave her permission to break so fully the discipline of our marriage. I pictured him as tall and lithe, as subtle and adept, someone British, perhaps, (though I could recall no one like this) whose austere humour and self-deprecating sophistication outmatched her own. But he could have been short and balding, for all I knew, the attraction something deeper, more mysterious. Whatever it was, it worked. At least temporarily. It lasted a few months, she told me. That invisible man thought he had her. As he took her hand once safely out of sight, once within the room (which I also had to imagine, the furnishings denied to me and therefore more powerfully imagined and hated, taking on a gloss of perfection that no real room could possibly have: all four-poster beds and proper chairs and a basin by the wall, though it might well have been a pitiable motel room with a too-soft bed and tiny bathroom with a mould-resistant white shower curtain and the requisite television perched, for want of space, on a stand attached to the wall), he thought that this was a beginning whose ending was uncertain, that she'd lost full control, that he'd set her loose into the music of her unfettered desire, that this thing he had started would have no shape, no form, would be without limits. That poor son of a bitch, I almost felt sorry for him.

We watched the hawks grow up. The two babies had long left the safety of their nest for adventures in flight. For a while, one of them (I called it Thing One) ran around the woodpile, doing test jumps and flights, then longer excursions with the mother and the other. They would fly over the nearby green belt, probably looking for an unsuspecting rodent with its nose to the ground. The mother would more often make solo trips for food. She flew overhead with a mouse or squirrel in its talons, once a snake dangling in the air, then release it to the young hawks, who sometimes perched on the garage, like a humanitarian airdrop over a starving village.

After a while I started to worry about Thing Two. It remained smaller, thinner than its sibling (I had no idea of their genders and could never get close enough to try to tell. Perhaps if Aaron returned . . .). I used Michael's binoculars to try to determine whether the smaller hawk was getting its share of food. Would the mother permit one of her children to starve?

When I went grocery shopping, I stopped in the pet-food aisle. What to feed a hawk? I walked up and down the aisle, scrutinising the options. Mostly dog and cat food in its seemingly infinite flavours and varieties, bags and cans, dry and moist. I'd never been a pet person, had rarely been in the aisle. I wondered whether some of the dog food might appeal — the packages said beef, duck, rabbit, though the pictures were of the happy dogs, not the unfortunate prey. I saw some bags of bird food, but these were not parakeets in a cage. This was stupid. I wasn't looking to feed a pet. Cans and bags, the very nature of the process, spoke of domesticity, centuries of devolution from a natural state of predation to ingratiation and dependency, the food as diluted as the blood lines. Wrong aisle. I pushed the cart to the meat section, walked up and down the length of the fridge, considering the chicken, the pork, sausages, ground beef. Predators need real meat. I decided on some inexpensive stewing beef, threw it into the cart along with some thick, flank steaks for the weekly barbecue with Geoff and Anna.

Geoff stood by as I placed the steaks on the grill. The weekly barbecue turned out to be an effective way to avoid work, to cut it short. I'd salted the slabs in the late morning — leaving them for a couple hours would tenderise the meat as it pushed moisture out, then let it sink back in. I'd sliced cucumber, tomato and onion for the salad, mixed an olive oil and balsamic vinaigrette, meticulously cleaned the grill, filled the barbecue with mesquite coal. It was more expensive than the briquettes, but it burned hotter. Later, I put garlic, olive oil, soy sauce, honey, and ginger in the blender, then placed the steaks into the marinade for several more hours. They'd have been happy with burgers.

Now, as I spoke with Geoff, I rubbed the steaks with a bit more salt and some pepper, laid them onto the grill. The sizzle and the rising scent prompted an immediate Pavlovian salivary response. I drank some beer, held the bottle up to the sunlight. Halfway through my second, light-headed now on an empty stomach. A shape moved behind, then past the bottle.

There it is, I said.

Geoff turned his head to follow the bottle I'd pointed to the sky.

Do you see it? I asked.

Geoff nodded. A beauty, he said.

The hawk was swooping in large arcs or circles, falling beyond sightline behind the tops of the pines, then returning. Hawks try to move, Michael had explained — having researched it thoroughly now — less by flapping their wings than by riding on rising air currents. They fly over land because that's where the air currents are. The smaller ones were starting now to do less flapping, more gliding, getting the hang of working with the world rather than always against it. I imagined what this might be like, wondered whether this meant a reliance less on intention than on the dynamic tension between intention and opportunity, allowing the direction and force of the currents determine organically the direction of flight so that flight was an interactive rather than purely directive activity, freedom the consequence of being less wilful, less determined, rather than more.

What are they eating? Geoff asked.

I told him about the rabbit. We hadn't seen the mother bring it into the yard but Michael had called us out back to take a look at the roof of the garage. The mum had laid or dropped the rabbit onto the roof, and all three gorged on the bloody mess.

A rabbit? Really?

A real rabbit — we saw it, I said. I flipped the thick steaks over, the smoke making Geoff's eyes tear.

He took a swallow of his beer. Wow, he said, big meal.

I told Talia about Michael's trip to the woods and we decided not to bother him about it, not to let on that we knew.

He's escaping us, she said.

I agreed with her. We agreed too that we had to ease the tension in the house but that we also needed to let him have his privacy. He was working hard. Meanwhile, we asked Michael only that he not stay out that late, that he give us some sense of when he would be home and that he make time for his regular piano practice. Michael agreed to that, and he stuck with his promise. He came home directly from his lesson, practised, had lunch, then went out for a while. He returned before dinner, practised some more.

What I didn't tell Talia is that I followed Michael one more time. I'm not sure why. I waited a few days, then when Talia went out — shortly after Michael took off — I took the bike and rode down to the path through the trees toward the creek. I left the bike by a tree near the road and walked this time. I could see the bike wheel trails in the dirt, hardened from lack of rain. I walked quietly, furtively.

There were two bikes on the ground. Michael sat on a rock by the creek as he'd done before. But beside him was Lewis. I hadn't realised he was back — he'd been taking various trips with his parents, to see grandparents but also to accompany his father on a research trip; his father was a scientist, an ecologist who had a field research project out west. Michael had been silent about Lewis.

Lewis was six months older than Michael and

about two inches taller. Adolescence was hitting him a bit more intensely, more quickly. Michael was wearing his shirt with the musical notes rising like balloons, a pair of blue shorts. Lewis wore cut-off jean shorts, a black T-shirt. They were sitting close, Michael's left knee touching Lewis's right. They were speaking, but I couldn't hear it over the distance, against the static of the river.

I saw, then, that they were holding hands. Lewis moved his head closer, and they kissed. It was a short kiss, shallow. They they let go, turning their heads away from each other, toward the river. Michael picked up a stone and tossed it into the water. Lewis did the same.

I walked as quietly as I could back along the path to my bike, pedalled home. By the time Talia returned, I was ensconced in my office.

Michael still out there somewhere? Talia asked.

As far as I know, I said.

It was the way that Geoff filled Talia's wine glass. I thought it over, then thought that I was overthinking. We'd all known each other for two decades. A long familiarity. Geoff actually met Talia a few weeks earlier than I did, though they'd only spoken a couple of times before he brought me to that party, where I'd struck up a conversation with Talia that went on and on through the evening, a conversation that had continued for years. The same party where he met Anna, the two women already close friends.

I remember watching the two of them, wines in hand, talking near the piano where only a few minutes before Talia had been playing. Geoff, of course, went up to speak with them, taking me along. I had been struck by Talia through that window, but found myself very aware of Anna, too. The shape of her face — she had a lean look, her jaw somewhat sharp, the outline softened by her hair. The four of us spent most of that party together, migrating from the lounge to the back porch, then to a circle of chairs on the lawn, the stars appearing. It felt things could go any way for a while, but then naturally evolved into our two couplings; Talia seemed to decide on me and I was drawn by her intensity. In the years after — Geoff and Anna married two years later, then Talia and I the next year — the four of us had taken many vacations together. A number of summer trips to the lake house Geoff's parents owned, a ski vacation that ended in a broken wrist, a number of camping trips, a joint trip to France when Anna had a conference and we'd all decided to go and turn it into two weeks — most of this before Michael came along. And of course the many days or evenings spent at one house or another. The friendship had had its waning moments, periods of greater distances, particularly when Michael was first born. The three of us, Talia and Michael and me, had gone into a cocoon mode during Michael's first year. We still saw Geoff and Anna, but the visits were fewer, truncated and perfunctory. I thought that the child had become a source of separation not just as a change in life circumstances that could not be wholly shared but also as a kind of tension, a reminder of the regret Anna had already started to feel.

It must have been hardest when Michael was a baby. Not just because this was a new thing — suddenly conversations were interrupted by cries, by Talia leaving the room to nurse, by diaper changes — and not just because this fifth person in the relationship became, inevitably, without our even wanting it to be, a gravity well, a dip in the fabric of space around them, so that thoughts and words and actions tumbled inevitably into it. *Michael slept four hours last night. As though you would know* — Talia turning to Geoff and Anna — *Stephen sleeps through most of it. Michael turned on his stomach on Monday and then, what a grouch, cried until I flipped him over.* We knew it must hurt Anna, but the words slipped from our lips, mine as much as Talia's, as difficult to stay away from the subject of a new child as from work or the weather. What else, for us, was there to talk about in those first months? More than this, more than the way Michael without meaning to, particularly that first year, became the centre of all things by displacing not just in time but importance all that seemed to occupy us before — the lawn went unmown, the small vegetable garden unweeded; it was all we could do to vacuum before we received visitors, and sometimes that went by the wayside, too. It was more than the way his sleep cycles and minor colds fenced what had been the sprawling field of our social lives, through which we had wandered unfettered for years, into discreet spaces to be planted or developed through will and intention. More than any of this, it must have been hard for Anna quite simply because Michael was an infant. It was the physical, undeniable fact of it. Here was a bawling, beautiful example of precisely what for Anna remained imagined, his birth drawing out even more fully her desire for a child, a making real of what for her remained intangible, unreachable, even as she said *May I?* and took a turn holding him carefully in her arms, rocked him as he cried, brushed what little hair he had with her fingers, inhaled his scent and without even realising it kissed him on the head between sentences. On the occasions when Geoff was handed Michael — always handed, never reached for — Anna observed him carefully, as though looking for counter-evidence. Anna and Geoff were displaced, awkward, sent to the margins for that year, but the friendship hadn't had enough time to deteriorate. It felt more like it had been frozen, and it thawed into something increasingly like what it had been as Michael grew into a boy, learned to walk and speak, though distances occurred now and again when jobs were particularly busy, when Talia and I were remodelling a bathroom and had little time for anything else. Sometimes I wanted more from Geoff, wanted him to be in some way more attentive to my life, to ask more questions. Geoff rarely asked about my writing, what I was working on, or when he did it was dutiful. I imagined Geoff might have other concerns about me, saw the irritation on Geoff's face when I made pronouncements on subjects Geoff knew better, or at least knew I was ignorant about. No one is everything to anyone. But for the most part, it was a lucky friendship. There was a thickness about it. We all knew who we were.

And yet I watched as Geoff kept his right arm casually around the back of my wife's chair while he leaned forward and with the other refilled her glass. Maybe it was the way he did this without asking, the way she responded by not responding at all, even to thank him. I tried to remember whether this was a new thing. It couldn't be. The long history of the friendship infused the pouring of that wine. Geoff had poured hundreds of glasses for Talia, for Anna, for me. Each of us had done the same. Geoff was just as likely to drape his well-wrought arm around the back of my chair if we found ourselves beside one another, wasn't he? I knew where this was coming from, knew too well I was oversensitive right now, prone to seeing signs and shadows everywhere. Talia had in some measure this summer become someone different, even if her indiscretion had occurred years before, and I was seeing through the lens darkly these days. I felt suspicion melt into embarrassment. Geoff looked up, seemed to notice my stare but without any discomfort.

More wine? he asked, raising his eyebrows and the bottle.

Did I reach for Anna, or she for me? This is what I think about, looking back on that hazy summer. So many drinks, so many evenings. Was it revenge on Talia? Am I that small-minded? Talia had sent me over to their house to drop off Anna's sweaters. She had brought each one over in anticipation of an evening growing cooler, draped it over a chair, but the evenings remained so warm she tended to forget them, and we'd accrued three. I was happy to get out of the house. Another excuse to leave my study, another way to avoid talking with Talia. Did I still have my suspicions about 'Rob'? I try to remember whether my suspicions began the moment her lips formed the name. When I'd insisted on a name — *You don't need to know who it was,* she'd argued — she'd finally said it, his name was Rob, a musician, *You didn't know him,* but hadn't she turned around slightly, not meeting my eyes? Hadn't she hesitated? I think I knew from that moment that she'd invented a name to salve my fury. And if she'd invented a name, I couldn't trust anything else she'd said, could I? Could I assume he was a musician? Could I assume I didn't know him? I'd called Anna ahead. She had made us a coffee in their living room, the kitchen still under construction. Take a look, she'd said. She was wearing tan shorts, bare feet, a T-shirt. Her hair was tied back. Weekend wear. Humid, hot, and the air conditioner was working hard. A plastic sheet hung over the doorway to the kitchen — the door itself removed — and it rippled in exhales of the nearby vent. She pushed it aside so we could enter, stood there with our coffee. Sunday, no workmen. The room had been stripped bare. It was the most honest a room can be. The gold linoleum had been removed, as had all the cabinets. Where the sink had been there was just a pipe running through the wall. The walls themselves had been stripped in some places past the wallboard, to the beams and spaces. It was just a room. It could be anything. A few pipes, some wires. The rest — countertop materials, cabinet knobs and drawer pulls, light fixtures, stainless steel appliances, all the things we think of, worry about, shop for — is theatre. It smelled of wood dust, though the builder had cleaned it pretty well.

She asked me about Michael, about his disappearances. I said that he went into the woods, to the creek, that I'd seen him there twice, but that I was sure it was a regular thing. He'd stopped staying there past dinner. He still came home to do his practising, but sometimes he disappeared again for a few hours, and I knew that's where he was going.

Why? she asked.

I said, Things are hard at home. He must feel it.

He's a sensitive boy. Kids know more than we think they do, more than we want to imagine.

I said, Have you guys thought more about . . .

She shook her head. We're still trying.

It can still happen, you're young still, I said. She nodded. She had tears on her face. I remember that there was nowhere to put the coffee. I looked around instinctively for a table or the counter that I knew had been dismantled, leaving only this empty room to fill with what might be imagined. Years later I would hear a story about an astronaut recently returned from a long trip in space, how he was using a hammer and when he was done, without thinking or looking, he simply moved his arm to set it in the air beside him, the gesture developed from his most recent experience, his hand's assumption that what he set aside into nothingness would remain there, afloat, available until he wanted it again. Our bodies develop new memories, adjust to circumstances. My mug was empty, and though it made the whole gesture seem too preconceived, awkward, I bent down to put it on the floor, took hers from her hand and did the same, then I put my arms around her. It was to comfort her. It was to say I was sorry that we had a son and they did not. It wasn't to reach for her in any other way, was it? Hadn't she looked at me before I did this? Hadn't she moved a step toward me? Yes, she had moved a step toward me, as unsure as I was what to do with the mugs, the one mug that said University of Virginia, which is where she spent four years, and the mug that had no letters, a handmade piece of pottery — yellow, blue — that she picked up somewhere and which matched nothing else. Didn't she look down, as she wept, and then look up at me, not with her head but just her eyes? Where does an embrace begin? Does it begin with a physical movement towards? Does it begin with a look? When does comfort become something else? There was just a bit of coffee still at the bottom of hers. Who picked them up later? Was it Geoff, was it her, was it a workman the next day? How strange but familiar the press of her lips. How odd it must have been to come across those mugs later, side by side on the floor.

All summer the hawk flew the length of the yard, landed on the patio table, perched on the chair.

Sometimes visible, sometimes invisible. It flew through our summer, carrying us through the heat and humidity, the varying degrees of weather that shaped our days. Michael in the backyard looking through his binoculars, bringing distance into focus. Talia and me, speaking but not speaking. Talking around a theme. The sounds of Michael playing, the notes rising and falling, audible, invisible. Talia and me, our argument visible but inaudible. How much did Michael sense?

The neighbours stopping by to see the hawk. The Gordons next door, with their daughter a few years older than Michael, quiet, probably not wanting to be there. She nods at Michael, who turns red. She mainly looks down, huddles into herself, tries not to exist. Shakes her head at the binoculars. *No, that's okay.* The Silvers across the street knocking at our door at nearly dusk.

We heard about the hawk, he says. In shape, tight polo shirt, slacks, gold ring on his pinkie. She looks like she's just back from tennis. He's got his camera, an expensive one. We take them through the house,

Pardon the mess, we're both working on books, you know how it is (thought they don't), then into the backyard. The hawk in the tree. The click of his camera. We'll drop by some prints.

Then Geoff and Anna at the door, in the foyer, in the backyard. Week after week. The phases of friendship. Visible, invisible. Good to see you, come in. Geoff in shorts, relaxed, pale blue short-sleeve shirt. For the first time he is getting older, the crow's feet starting to imprint around his eyes, the skin bunched at his elbow, silver threads on his chest. Anna in a skirt, her hair tied back, a kiss on Talia's cheek, a kiss on mine. Thank god for Geoff and Anna. A beer, a second beer, Geoff and I on the patio chairs, the sky starting to darken. The hawk invisible, deep in a tree or off on a hunt, but who cares. The silence of predators. Anna and Talia a few yards away, on the lawn, wine glasses in hand. Talia more relaxed than I've seen her all summer. Me too. A third beer. Talia and Anna back on the patio chairs. Anna brushing a bug from her leg, putting her hair around her ear. Talia's red hair, curly, barely controlled. Our words slipping past each other. Interrupted stories. Anna and Geoff looking at each other, looking away. All summer, Geoff and Anna in the living room, on the deck, in the backyard, on the patio. Brushing up in the dark of a stairwell. Not here, stop, Michael two rooms away, the patio door open, the sounds of Bach, of Beethoven, of Brahms slipping through the screen. A missed button on a blouse. All summer the hawk swooping around the notes. All summer, the notes climbing, descending, hovering as though in uncertainty, the hawk perching, a moment, here, then gone, did it happen, the morning come quickly, head under the pillow, the rattle of Michael pulling out his bike, the closing of a door, the aroma of coffee.

THREE

How long had they been going to Hotel Gerrard?

When Michael died. Talia was already showing significant declines, wading in the shallows of Lethe. Michael's death pushed her deeper into forgetfulness. I picture her in the weeks before his death, as she tried so hard to remain tethered to her sanity, someone hanging from a windowsill above Alzheimer's vertiginous depths, gripping onto the edge of the sill with whitened knuckles. And when I came to the window to tell her the news, she let go. Maybe I should have withheld it from her longer. Maybe I blamed her and was being cruel.

I listen to Sonata 30 over and over, as though it might bring me closer to understanding Talia, even as her mind drifts further away. I don't think this work is meant to show off his genius, which is the impression, right or wrong, that I get sometimes from Mozart.

Despite the astonishing virtuosity of his embellishments, Beethoven seems not just to be going for a profundity of feeling but to be asking deeper questions of the sonata form and of us: Where does the sonata end? Is the sonata a form or a basis for improvisatory wandering? I think I can see this in the second movement, a slow movement but an angry one — the division between first and second movement not the expected one of fast then slow but instead of peace then disruption. I can hear the structure-within-structure: the introduction of a fugue as one of six variations in the third movement. The fugue itself is, of course, a structure of multiple voices and this structure within structure would seem to use the very aspect of sonata form that we expect — variation, recapitulation (that is, repetition and return) — to burst it apart at its seams.

Is it wrong of me to wait until the third act to introduce a new character? Geoff and Anna did finally get the child they hoped for, in the spring following what we came to refer to as our Summer of the Hawks. When their son was born that April, they called him Bede. It means prayer, and it did seem like theirs was answered. The odds had seemed so against them. They brought him to our house, the little larva wrapped in blankets and wearing a tiny blue hat. Michael, at thirteen, seemed interested, but as from a distance.

I don't believe in divine intervention, Geoff said, holding the bundle, but still, I can see why they are called miracles. I remember Anna wore an expression that was difficult to parse. She scooped Bede from Geoff's arms, and the baby moved his eyes towards her.

You can use our room, Talia said.

Your redemption fantasies, Talia called my novels. I find myself trying to figure out what it is I want from Orville, who is starting to see, not just feel, the effects of his treatment. Orville knows for sure the drugs are affecting his outer appearance when Rebecca, the clinic receptionist, starts to actually see him. He's felt the inner changes for weeks — the increased energy, the more powerful sensations, deeper and less disturbed sleep at night. The outer changes seem real to him, but it is more difficult to be certain. He knows from many years of experience the way his brain can reinterpret his body image in the mirror. When he was in his early forties, he went through a period of weight gain. He got fat. Too much time at work, too much fast food because he left so early and never had the gumption to make his lunch the night before. He'd been between exercise regimes and his metabolism had changed. He gained seven kilos before he really could admit it. He'd look at his body in the mirror, after a shower, and realise he was a bit heavier. His clothes were tighter. But it wasn't until he saw a photo Gina took at the beach, a trip they took with Gina's sister and her husband — Orville was leaning over to help his nephew build a sandcastle, his gut hanging out — that he was shocked into recognition. So though he could see now his hair thickening and regaining some of its natural colour — dark brown — he has been distrustful of his judgement about his own appearance, less certain about what seemed to him more taut skin around his neck, fewer wrinkles around his eyes and something more difficult to pin down, a kind of sharpening of his features, as though being sculpted out of a block of flesh, the way Michelangelo said the figures he created were already in the stone, which he simply had to chip away to reveal.

Somewhere there is a photographic record of his changes, video as well. The nurses take pictures of him each week. They take pictures of his face from the front, both profiles. They take pictures of the top of his head, behind his head. They take full-body photographs that require him to be almost naked. Orville has never thought to ask to see those photographs but, now that the changes have started to accumulate, have become visible, he suddenly wants to see them, to have documentation of the changes, an objective record of what he believes is happening to him. Without Gina, there is no one he can ask to do it.

But he realises the changes must be real because Rebecca *looks* at him now when he checks in at the clinic. The first time he came in, she barely glanced up from her computer screen and, when she did, her smile was polite — cool and quick. Her eyes had barely met his. But now, as when the jogger nodded to him on the path a couple weeks before, he is becoming visible. It is not a sudden return to visibility but as though he is fading into the world in stages, first for some people and then for others. He appeared young enough that the jogger saw him as a legitimate thing in the world. Now he apparently is looking young and vibrant enough to be noticed as a male in the species by a woman as young as Rebecca. He figures he must look in his early fifties now. This must have been how he faded out of the world, how he grew invisible, in stages. He remembers being aware that women were no longer looking at him. First of course it was young women, those in their twenties, then gradually women in their thirties, forties and fifties. Men, too, gradually started looking at him differently. Less as a potential rival, more as someone to treat with polite respect. At some point, the chance of pissing off another man at a bar, on the subway, at an intersection — something that could lead to words or worse — became slight, then turned to zero. But all of that happened slowly. This, the reverse ageing, is occurring much more quickly, at a pace of months rather than years. Orville recalls a time-lapse film of a sunflower growing, the leaves and stem lengthening, bud forming and blossoming. What took weeks suddenly took seconds, and what would have gone unnoticed was suddenly clear and real. The effect of the drug is like that. He is on time-lapse reverse ageing. He is re-blooming.

Good morning, Orville, Rebecca says.

She is smiling at him. It is nothing like flirtation. He is still, in her eyes, too old for that. But it is the kind of warmth that she is not even aware she reserves for a man at least on the outer edge of his prime. She's taken, over the past couple of weeks, without invitation, to calling him by his first name.

Good morning, Orville responds. New haircut?

She touches her hair, which is not just shorter but straighter. It frames her face, gives it a pleasing, angular appearance, seems to heighten her cheekbones.

Yes, she says. At least someone noticed.

Did someone *not* notice?

My stupid boyfriend, of course.

I think perhaps you need a new boyfriend.

This very exchange, the time she's taken to talk with him, her eyes on his, rather than on the screen, would not have been possible two months ago. He still looks old enough for the conversation to be in large measure avuncular. She will take the comment as a legitimate compliment, as an implicit but chaste flirtation on his end.

Oh, he's lost some points, Rebecca says with a laugh, that's for sure.

It's not just her interaction with him that's changed, though. He is more aware of her. Not that he wasn't struck by her the first time he came to the clinic. But he has a stronger bodily awareness of her. His body is responding to her presence more powerfully. He eyes the skin on her neck, the light blond fuzz over the fullness of her lips. He is loathe to end the conversation.

So long as you're keeping a record, Orville says.

She laughs again, checks him in, and he sits down. He chooses a seat near the receptionist's desk, watches as she speaks on her headset. He watches the way she sits up on some calls, leans back in her chair to speak on others, which tells him whether it is professional or personal. He watches her on occasion watch him watching.

Soon Michael took an interest in Bede. I wasn't expecting a new baby, then toddler, to be of particular interest to a thirteen-year-old. But Michael was attentive. He would sit by Bede's high chair, Michael's old high chair, brought down from the attic when Anna and Geoff came to visit. *I suppose there was a reason I never got rid of this*, Talia said to me, as though to excuse one of the few visible manifestations of her usually hidden sentimental side. And he would make faces at Bede, funny noises, or hold out Bede's plastic blue and green rattle, shaking it to get his attention. Eventually, Bede noticed and started to smile. It was pretty early on that Bede used Michael's name, though he first pronounced it (and for some time) 'Mile'. Even when crawling, he would say 'Mile, Mile' and follow Michael around the living room rug, down the hall. Michael tolerated it, even seemed to like it, and later, when Bede started to walk, he would pull Michael by the hand when we visited to show him a toy or new game in his room. Talia had private regrets, I think, that we never had a second child. She seemed to enjoy watching them. I'd see her following the boys with her eyes, *The toddler leading the teen, like brothers*, as Talia put it.

Even during Talia's illness it could be difficult to get hold of Michael. This became a typical scenario when I would call: At the fifth ring, as I'd prepare to hang up before going to voicemail, Jacob would answer.

It's Stephen.

Hi, Stephen. How are you? How is Talia?

She's okay. She recognised me for a few minutes today.

I'm sorry.

Jacob moved in with Michael in Manhattan several years earlier, and he is a truly compassionate man. I've wondered how long he can remain a public defender. Jacob has the pedigree for a much more lucrative career (Harvard) and the job's demands on his psyche — he has always struck me as the more vulnerable, as much less able to suppress his feelings than Michael — will surely grow intolerable. But maybe he shows a different side, a harder one, on the job.

Thanks, Jacob. I was wondering whether Michael was around.

Sorry, Stephen. I know he's gotten your messages, but he is very busy. He's hardly been here this month.

I understand. Would you just let him know I called again?

Of course I will. Please give Talia my love.

As I'd hang up (recognising suddenly how that phrase dates me — it remains to my mind quite literal, a physical action), I could picture Jacob, a young man in a close-shaven red beard, standing at the kitchen counter, writing a note with his left hand, the phone still in his right. Michael, whenever he comes home, will toss the note into a pile of notes and envelopes and flyers that Jacob will meticulously go through at the end of the week. Michael will pour himself a glass of chardonnay, kiss Jacob, then do whatever it is that he does in the few hours he is not, in one sense or another, working. I try to remember what that was. Read? Watch television? That is, at least, how I imagine it, on the basis of my recollections of the last time Talia and I stayed with Michael at the apartment he shares with Jacob. This was two years ago, in September, just before travelling became too difficult for Talia, too overwhelming. Even during that trip, she on occasion gripped my arm. Talia, who had always led the way, whose sense of direction (*We can go that way, Stephen, but as it's north, we will be walking quite a long time*) had always been as unerring as her taste (*Seriously, Stephen, with loafers?*), her sense of etiquette (*You're not going to email a thank you note, Stephen*). She gripped my arm, let me guide her — not along the most efficient route, no doubt — along the streets, in the airport. Things had not deteriorated yet to the point where I had to accompany her constantly. But when I came out of the airport restroom before the return flight, she had a look of panic on her face. She stood with her back against the wall, gripping her small shoulder bag, her jaw clenched.

Where have you been, she hissed.

Just the restroom, I said.

I know that, she said. She was still trying to cover, even from me, even though she was aware I knew. She said, I simply meant you were taking quite a long time;

we need to get through security. Do you want us to miss our plane?

I didn't remind her that Michael had dropped us hours early because he needed to be at a rehearsal, that we still had quite a while before boarding started, that we'd just been discussing how to spend the time, perhaps at one of the bookstores.

I'm sorry, I said, and meant it in every way one might imagine.

I've described Geoff and Anna as our oldest friends, our best friends. In the long arc, that is true. But, as I mentioned, there were periods of retraction, and Bede's birth led to the longest of them. I suppose it was inevitable that despite the greater connection we now had with Geoff and Anna — all of us now parents — and a great ease between the two boys, a sense that Michael was taking on the role of protector, a distance would form as well. Anna and Geoff were in a very different parenting place, one of little sleep and careful attention. We had seen their world but no longer lived in it, and their social life became more tied to Bede's, with birthday parties and play groups, with the parents of Bede's friends in school. We saw them less for a period of some years, the growing-up years, lost years.

We understood how intense those growing up years could be. It was certainly true with Michael. Keeping up with his phases could at times take a great deal of our attention and emotional energy. When Michael was seven, for example, he became obsessed with floods and boats. For months, when it rained particularly hard, he worried that our house would be carried off. When he went grocery shopping with Talia or with me, he would insist we load the cart with extra supplies *just in case*, and to satisfy him, we created an emergency bin with cans of tuna and beans, bottles of juice and water, a torch, a radio, blankets, extra clothes (those he disliked, which he culled from his dresser). We put it in the basement, but he protested immediately that this was the first part of the house that would get flooded, which was hard to argue with, though we'd never had a flood in the basement in the decade we'd been there. So we moved it to the attic.

That's where we'll end up, Michael said.

It started when he listened to a recording of Stravinsky's *The Flood*, a musical play based on the biblical story of Noah. Michael was well into classical music by then, and Talia had taken it out of the collection for him after he returned home from Sunday school talking about Noah's ark. I suppose you could say his obsession began with the Sunday school lesson, but I think it was the intensity of the Stravinsky recording (which I heard for the first time with Michael) that did it.

Michael came home from Sunday school that day with a picture he'd drawn of the ark, a Noah figure on top — stick-like, wearing what seemed to be a robe — two animals next to him, whose varieties were hard to discern, and a line of even more ambiguously designated animals stretching behind the boat. He'd drawn storm clouds above the boat and little marks of rain coming down. He arrived at noon — we took turns with two other families doing drop-off and pick-up, and this was our lazy Sunday — running up the path with his drawing in hand. Michael was a very sincere boy. He thought hard about things. During lunch, after he described the flood, the animals and — he was indignant on this point — the fact that no one believed him (*No one, Dad — he built the ark and people said he was crazy*), Talia said she had a surprise. We dutifully filed into the living room, where she went to cabinet that held our record collection (lovingly compiled before the popularity of CDs) and pulled out the Stravinsky album. Michael was disappointed with the album cover (mainly words, with no pictures of Noah), but he listened to it that afternoon and then again after dinner.

That night, as it happened, we had a hard rain. At two in the morning we found him beside our bed — he always went to his mother's side when he was disturbed — in tears.

Mummy, the flood is coming.

It's just a regular old rain, Talia said.

It doesn't seem a coincidence that Talia and I were going through a very hard period, suppressing our arguments (largely) in front of Michael, trying to keep our angry voices low in the bedroom when he was asleep. We alternated periods of cold silence with late night fights, and I remember we'd had one of those that night so were already short on sleep. She picked him up — he was small for his age, but at seven it was becoming an effort — and carried him back to his bed.

Two hours later, he was back, crying. Check on Angus, he said, referring to our dog, only a year old.

So we all got up at 4 am to check on the dog, who was all too happy to see us and started barking, thinking optimistically that it was morning. Michael gave the dog a hug, then ran over to the living-room curtains, which he parted and knelt between to watch the rain. Angus sat with him. At that stage, we were all wide awake. I made us cheese omelettes with toast — normally a Saturday breakfast — and we brought in the morning with some music (Vivaldi, not the Stravinsky, which we buried in the cabinet, the only acknowledgement by Talia that perhaps she'd made a strategic error) and watched as the rain dwindled to drizzle, then stopped. Michael kept an umbrella in his backpack for several months. He spent every morning after a rain looking for rainbows, keeping his eye out for them through the car window as we drove him to school, seeking some sort of promise that all would be okay. This continued on and off for several months, whenever we had hard rains, throughout the tough period that our marriage eventually weathered.

When Orville comes into the clinic the next week, he gives a quick hello to Rebecca, who makes sure not to look at him too long. Neither of them knows whether there is any official prohibition on their relationship. No one had said anything to her at the start. Maybe because she isn't part of the medical staff. Maybe no one had really thought it through. What were the chances a twenty-seven-year-old woman was going to start a physical relationship with an old man? But it seemed likely to raise concerns. Rebecca doesn't want to lose her job. Orville doesn't want to get kicked out of the trial. Both of them, he thinks, are also a little embarrassed.

Looking good, the doctor says when Orville has been called back and put through his paces — blood pressure, muscle tone, physical reactions, balance, photographs. How are you feeling?

Great. Young.

Well, technically you are, the doctor says.

How young now?

As I've said before, no two people are the same at any age, the doctor says, but there are trends. If I didn't know better, based on your looks and your stats, I'd peg for you a man in his upper-thirties, excellent condition.

Orville thinks for a moment. He says, I've been wondering.

How young will you get?

That's right.

Well, this is all a bit unexpected. We hadn't antici-pated such a strong whole-body response."

Does that mean . . . ?

No, you're not going to do a Benjamin Button. No turning into an infant. You'll stabilise soon. We'll see to that. We're actually not sure how far back we can take you, but to be conservative, we'll stop the treatments long before your body faces adolescence, if such a reverse is even possible.

Mid-twenties?

An outside chance. Probably you'll level out with stats that put you around thirty. That good enough?

Orville asks, What then?

The doctor looks uncomfortable. Well, he says, we did say this was an experiment. Our expectation is that you'll then age normally. Barring accident or serious illness, at this point we believe you'll get to live those years again.

What the doctor didn't say, but Orville hears, is *And do it right.*

Like brothers, then not. Michael did what teenagers do. He was still deeply involved in piano — more and more — so didn't have a normal childhood, exactly. But he became absorbed in his own social scene. It wasn't until Bede was in high school, Michael in his twenties and well into his career that we started to see Geoff and Anna regularly again. By then, the stresses of raising Bede had eased. Father and son had their tensions; Bede seemed more interested in writing and English than following Geoff into the sciences, but it wasn't that, exactly, that caused the distance between them. Bede was an introvert, where Geoff was an extrovert.

I wish he would just do something, Geoff said once, a few months after we started to see each other regularly again.

What would you have him do? I asked.

Not sit there, in his room, hour after hour. Join a team. Perform. Volunteer. Go to a party now and then.

Geoff stopped talking then, cocking his ear toward the stairs.

Here he comes, Geoff said. Probably needs sustenance.

As though on cue, Bede came down the stairs — Geoff must have been attuned to the sounds of his house, the shifting of a door, the turning down of music. I watched Bede nod to his father and to me, then head — as Geoff predicted — for the kitchen. He was a bit smaller than Michael, smaller-boned, or maybe it was finer boned. He took more after Anna than Geoff, even physically. He didn't have Geoff's ease in the world. Bede walked somewhat awkwardly. I empathised: His life would not be the Zen affair of his father's, for whom so much seemed to come with few obstacles. He wasn't as lithe as Geoff, Bede's face squarer, his hair dark. I heard him open and close some cupboards, the fridge. Then he was back, walking up the stairs with a plate of something.

See what I mean, Geoff said.

In the introduction, Talia's manuscript recounts speculations about the influence of Beethoven's life on his art. Foremost his gradual and then profound deafness. In 1802 he wrote a letter to his brothers while staying in a village near Vienna. The document, a sort of will, has been called the Heiligenstadt Testament after the name of the village. In that short letter, he reveals how much his growing deafness cost him. He finds himself isolated, frustrated, driven nearly to suicide. It is only sheer willpower and a dedication to his music that stays his hand. As for death, he writes:

> *If he comes before I have had the opportunity of developing all my artistic powers, then, notwithstanding my cruel fate, he will come too early for me, and I should wish for him at a more distant period; but even then I shall be content, for his advent will release me from a state of endless suffering. Come when he may, I shall meet him with courage.*

He lived another quarter century to produce music beyond imagining, including his final sonatas. We find courage where we can.

Technically, the sonata is a movement, not a form. The sonata movement is often the first in a three- or four-movement piece for a solo instrument like the piano, so the piece itself is often referred to by the same name, or the first movement is awkwardly called the sonata-form-movement. The movement begins with an exposition, where the music's themes, its main tunes, are introduced, are 'exposed'. The exposition typically has two parts, one in the primary key called the tonic and the other usually in the dominant key. (*The tonic is the first note of a scale, the dominant the fifth note,* Talia explained. So if you start in one key, you can create a contrasting key based on the dominant note in that scale. That's as far as I can understand it.) The next part of the movement is the development, where the themes are expanded, modified, made more complex. The movement ends with a recapitulation, which repeats — in a new, varied way — the exposition. The form is all about, as Leonard Bernstein has said (quoted by Talia), balance and contrast. There is a balance among three movements. But there is a contrast between themes built on the tonic and those built on the dominant. A composer might tease us by staying for quite a while in the dominant during the final recapitulation but, ultimately, he returns us to the tonic, to the key that started the piece. If you play the tonic, then play the dominant and then stop, there is a sense of something incomplete, unfinished, in need of resolution. Moving to the dominant key is like going away, setting off for vacation, university, career. Returning to the tonic is, musically, like coming home.

I'm trying to remember the last time Michael and Bede met. A decade or more, what with Michael living in New York and Bede having gone to university in Michigan and staying out there. But he remained close with his parents, particularly Anna, who kept Talia informed in some detail about Bede's life. Bede had in the end become a technical writer, so had in a sense married his tendencies with Geoff's interests.

He's come home recently, too late for Michael's funeral. After Geoff died — a stroke, unexpected — he returned to help out Anna. He lives a few minutes' drive away from her and despite Geoff's concerns, Anna tells me Bede has a fairly active social life — friends, dating.

You should see him, she said the last time she came by to take Talia out for a couple of hours.

Yes, I said, we should arrange that sometime.

Orville wakes beside Rebecca, looks at her and immediately feels desire, followed closely by guilt and remorse. He tells himself, I've done nothing wrong. Rebecca is sleeping on her left side, facing him. Her hair covers part of her face. She sleeps so quietly he has to watch her torso moving to persuade himself she is breathing. The sheet half-covers her, revealing a naked leg, curled up toward her stomach. He hasn't had a night like the previous one in a long time, years and years, since the early days of his marriage. He regrets none of it. Still, he can't shake the feeling he's in some sense betrayed Gina, gone four years now. He'd been with only her for forty years. Was five years enough time? How long is enough? Fifteen per cent? Twenty? If the drug hadn't increased his libido, he'd have been able to stand the loneliness. Not that it would have been easy. But it would have been a dull ache, rather than this need, this urgency that — having been absent, he can see it as something distinct from himself — takes on the character of a burden.

If she wakes beside him, he'll be drawn inexorably back for yet more of what his body, even now, wants. His body — this new body emerging from within the old one, literally shedding his skin. It has been decades, and his past decades are now, as has been said, a foreign country: What is the protocol here, the etiquette? How insulted will she be to find he's gotten out of bed? He sits up slightly to see her bedside clock. Nearly nine, Saturday morning.

He slips from the sheets as carefully as he can, slowly and gently to avoid waking her, the way he used to try to avoid waking Gina, who was always a late sleeper. Perhaps if he makes some breakfast, that gesture will make up for this small abandonment. In the bathroom, he stops to examine his face. Forty? He needs a shave, the stubble mostly black, only a few subtle hints of grey. In the few months on this drug, this jaw line has gradually been chiselled out of the familiar jowls of his face. He's noticed that gym workouts have much greater effects, biceps, pecs and shoulder muscles responding faster and more powerfully to the weights, heart rate calming on the treadmill, gut flattening, though he's certainly eating a lot more, voraciously.

As usual in the mornings now, he's famished. Rebecca lives in a one-bedroom condo that Orville guesses was built in the seventies. He hadn't been much interested in the surroundings last night when they came in at nearly eleven, both more than tipsy, but now, in the daylight — a top floor, with a cathedral ceiling and a skylight that invites the morning sunshine into the living room — he looks around. It's been renovated at least once, probably in the mid-nineties to judge by the fixtures, the faux-granite counter in the kitchen, but it still has the seventies-style brick fireplace wall. The kitchen itself is galley-style. A bowl of fruit on the counter. The fridge is stocked with eggs, bread for toast. Rummaging through the cabinets, worried at every clunk and crash that he'll wake her, he finds an eight-inch non-stick omelette pan. It feels good, even in someone else's kitchen, to be cracking and beating eggs, cooking an omelette with the butter, garlic and some cheddar he found deep in a drawer, the cheese half-opened and hardened but fine for melting.

Rebecca walks in as he finishes cooking the omelette, which he carefully folds. She has a on light robe, pale red, which she cinches tighter as she walks over, running her hand through her hair and scooping it over her right ear.

Hey, she says.

Hey back.

You found the kitchen.

Hope I didn't wake you.

Smells good.

He plates the omelette, conscious now of an audience, adds a piece of toast, two thin slices of orange. She's staring, still standing there, as though it were his kitchen and she the stranger, so he walks over to her, puts his hand gently on her waist. He's in strange territory. It's funny — he has decades more living than she does, but this is her territory. He's been in a sense thrown forward through time, and in this strange culture of the young he doesn't know which moves to make, what is expected, what would offend. He goes for something old-fashioned and hopes it's a classic. More than a domestic peck, less than an invitation.

Good morning, he says.

She seems to relax, then.

Good morning yourself, she says. I'll make some coffee.

Don't bother — I'll do it. This omelette's for you. Eat it while it's hot. I'll make another.

The coffee's in the cabinet to the left of the fridge, she says, second-to-top shelf.

As he scoops out the coffee, he watches from the corner of his eye as she takes a seat at the dining room table, tries a forkful.

What a treat, she says.

Sorry there's no sprig of parsley. It's my signature.

Your signature. So basically this is your thing, she says, making eggs the next morning.

I haven't had a 'next morning', the way you mean it, in forty years.

I can see there are advantages to old men.

He puts down the eggs he planned to crack, walks over to her. She is looking up at him, egg on her chin. Her eyes have a question in them. He'd forgotten this. The fragility of insecurity, that she does not yet know who she is, has not come to grips with certain realities. He touches her cheek, puts his head down to her. This time it's a long kiss. It tastes of morning and egg. He finds himself kneeling beside her (his knees don't complain!) kissing her longer, hand drawn to her leg, exposed again, half out of the robe.

You're not hungry? she says, pulling away slightly.

He leans forward to close the distance, puts his lips to the smooth, taught skin of her neck.

Starved, he says.

A form is never a straitjacket. The great sonata composers in the classical period — Mozart, Haydn — played with the form at various times and in various ways, starting with what might be expected then teasing us, moving us away from where we thought we were going. There is no recipe, Talia once old me. It's not that there is a Platonic sonata to which composers try to adhere. It's more the other way. This was a time in our marriage when we were very close, when she was teaching me about music, on and off for a few years before Michael was born and then when he was just a small boy. While he slept down the hall, we would spend the evening in the living room. I wanted to understand music as she understood it in order to understand her. She would put on a record, and we would lie on our backs beside one another on the rug in front of the stereo. She started, as I recall, with Bach, with the fugue. Gradually, she gave me an education on the shift from baroque to classical to romantic to modern. Again and again, she would ask me to listen, then she would point out a shift in theme or movement or simply feeling. When I had trouble hearing it, as I often did, she would say, *Listen to this again* — would lift the phonograph needle and carefully replace it so that I could hear it once more.

What do you mean by 'It's more the other way', I asked.

She said, Forms arise from composers, rather than composers following forms. The definitions, the generic structures, these are developed afterwards. They become, eventually, a kind of ghost architecture, a place to start, not to end, an expectation from which to improvise, to surprise. Limitations are in the imagination, not the music. Beethoven, Haydn's greatest student, took the sonata to places even his teacher could not have imagined.

Orville looks over his beer at Reg. It turns out that Reg was a better-looking older man than he is a younger one. Reg has lost his paunch, shaved his beard. But instead of making him seem lighter, the effect is the opposite. The age-softened features have disappeared and his nose is birdlike now. His cheeks have sunk into his face. He looks more severe. He's given up glasses, and his eyes — a sharp green — dart around more often, as though there is some place he needs to be, someone else he needs to see, or as though he expects someone he dislikes or fears will enter the room. He looks a lot smaller, as though the loss of physical years has taken away the bravado built from experience as well. Like Orville, he's gotten thin enough to need new clothes, and it is just as well. Like Orville's, Reg's old clothes — his generic khaki shorts, his bright-patterned shirts with an extra button undone — would fit his new age as poorly as they would his new frame. Reg wears a pair of jeans, the skinny type that Orville has seen but can't quite get himself to wear, at least not yet. He's not as thin as Reg. Orville knows he doesn't look as young as Reg, either — along with the weight, Reg seems to have dropped off the years much faster. The doctor's assurances to the contrary, Reg could pass for late twenties. Reg isn't just getting a second youth; he is disappearing into it.

Reg is also wearing a flannel plaid shirt, fitted. Orville recognises it from the Gap — he'd gone there himself with Rebecca. She'd insisted on taking him to the mall.

We'll start with the Gap, she said, because it's easy, before we do anything radical. He didn't know what she meant by radical. He'd felt uncomfortable enough at the Gap, among all the younger people, until it dawned him that the kid folding the shirts and putting them on the rack, the one who'd asked him if he needed some help, saw him as just another youngish guy.

I'm okay for now, he said.

Alright, the young man had responded with a smile, let me know if you need anything.

Rebecca had picked out some clothes. She'd taken away his belt, which he'd owned for some fifteen years — she held it out with distaste and tossed it into the trash — and chosen another.

Reg is just plain skinny and looks to Orville a bit strung out. It has been three weeks since they'd seen each other last — at the clinic — and that's turned out to be years in terms of appearances. Orville wonders how different he looks in Reg's eyes.

How goes the plumbing business? Orville asks.

Reg shakes his head. I did a little work for a buddy, a guy who used to work for me. Has his own business now.

Didn't go well?

Not really.

What happened?

He treated me like I didn't know what the hell I was doing. He kept explaining, kept too close an eye on me, kept questioning my decisions. More than that, he spoke curtly, harshly.

Reg had finally reminded the guy that he in fact used to be his boss, that he had a decade's more experience and to leave him the hell alone. His friend told him to get lost.

He looked at me, Reg says, and he saw a kid. He knew who I was. He knew what I had done. But he couldn't get past it. He saw what he saw.

Orville asks, Was it what you looked like or just the fact that you're changing?

I don't know, Reg says. Maybe that was part of it. Maybe it freaked him out or pissed him off. Maybe it was too strange for him to take. To be honest, I don't have that many old friends. But the couple I do have, who I told about this, look at me in a way that's hard to explain.

Like you're a freak, Orville says.

You've gotten that, too.

Orville has. Like Reg, he doesn't have a lot of old friends. A few have died. A number have moved away to be somewhere warmer, Florida or Arizona, or to some other state to be closer to their kids and grandkids, or just moved to another part of town, to a smaller place, a condo or even, in one case, a retirement community. Before Gina died, their social circle had narrowed to only a few couples, whom they saw for the occasional dinner, a monthly concert. They kept up with Orville for a while after she'd gone, had invited him out. But that has faded, mainly. Orville knows he's a lot to blame for that. There were a couple of people he'd sometimes see at the gym. Not friends, certainly not old ones. Just a couple guys he'd speak with. They would go out for lunch now and again. They noticed he was changing, and though he explained he was in an experimental medical treatment, they would make comments about it and then started to make excuses after the workouts. They had to get home, had to catch up with their kids, whatever. Orville had in fact recently changed to another gym, one on the other side of town where no one knows him.

Anyway, Reg says, I'm, as they say, rethinking my long-term goals.

In what sense?

I spent one lifetime crawling into tight spaces, fixing toilets, coming home late or getting call-outs. Maybe I'll spend this next one doing something else.

This next one. It was something Orville hadn't thought about closely. He realised now it was something he had pushed away from his thoughts, hadn't wanted to face. If he was heading toward thirty, he could have another fifty years ahead of him. Half a century to do something with. Half a century, he thought, to pay for. Thanks to Gina's sharp financial skills, he had a good chunk of money set aside, but not enough for half a century. He'd need to earn money again. He was sitting down at a two-top with Reg at happy hour. But he felt dizzy, disoriented. Exhausted at the thought of all those years ahead. It had all happened so quickly. Orville felt like he'd taken a walk and found himself standing over a sudden precipice, the soil unstable beneath his feet, the wind pressing at his back.

Michael's so angry with me, Stephen. But you'd think he'd come.

I am so absorbed in Orville, it takes me a moment to realise Talia is speaking clearly to me, nearly about the present. I'm at the breakfast table. Fifteen years ago, we knocked down the wall separating the kitchen from the back porch, then glassed it in as an extension. One of my books had done very well — by literary novel standards — and the royalties, though not exorbitant, had paid for the renovation. Talia called it, in her way of rolling appreciation within irony, the literary wing. Small but serviceable. We often ate breakfast in that conservatory, which stands on the south side of the house and gets so warm in the sunshine that even in winter we have to open a window. She had been sitting quietly, staring through the glass at the oak, whose leaves were full red and starting to puddle around the yard.

Now she looks at me expectantly, her eyes clear, as though we were in the middle of a conversation.

You know who I am.

You know I love you, Stephen, but don't be an ass. I don't know how long I have.

Why is Michael angry at you?

I didn't say he was angry.

You did.

I wish he'd come.

You know how busy a pianist's life can be.

Busy.

Rehearsals, recordings, tours.

Don't patronise me.

I'm just relaying the information

You're trying to make an old lady feel better.

He'd come around if he could.

He's leaving it a bit late.

Don't say that.

Let's not start lying to each other now.

You've been his world from the start. Mine, too, of course.

Grow up. How's my book?

Beautifully written, as usual.

Please.

And as usual I'm struggling through some of the music lingo and the notations.

And as usual you'll do fine. Just make it look like I was of sound mind when I wrote it. Eliane will double-check the technical material.

Talia, why did you say Michael is angry at you?

Just be sure to pick him up early. There's school tomorrow. You know how grumpy he gets.

Yes, of course. Look at the beautiful oak leaves.

The oak leaves truly are particularly brilliant this year. I think about a book on our shelf, *1000 Places to See Before You Die*. I bought it for Talia's sixtieth birthday. I suppose it was a bit morbid for a birthday gift: She mocked me — *Counting down?* she asked — but she read through it and marked some pages. It's well-thumbed, if not as well travelled as I would like. A thousand is a big number and, on reflection, it is obviously the kind of book best given as a university graduation present. We made it to a few over the next few years, though, before Talia's problems began, or at least before we could no longer ignore them. One place the list did inspire us to visit, or really finally revisit, was Aspen. We had lived in Colorado for decades but hadn't made the trip in nearly as long, not being skiers. We drove the four-and-a-half hours through the mountains in autumn. Perfect for us, as the rates are best then, though hardly cheap. Some good restaurants, but I didn't think much of the town, which now seemed overly designed to serve New Yorkers with too much money who wanted a break from their places in Connecticut or Martha's Vineyard. Talia called me a reverse snob when I made my observations; maybe she's right. But the views — the aspen trees turn a gorgeous yellow. We took a free nature hike with a guide.

People come from all over to see the leaves change, a dozen of us on this walk: groups from California, Arkansas, Maine, a couple with their baby from Italy, another group of three from France. Talia walked ahead of me in the new hiking boots she'd purchased for just this purpose. It was chilly when we started in the morning, but by 11 am it was warm enough that she unzipped the bottom of her hiking pants (stuffing them into her backpack, a very old purchase that she declined to replace despite a tricky zipper and the fraying straps). Even at sixty-two her calves were shapely and strong. She'd long stayed in shape at the gym and kept up easily with the young guide through a few switchbacks. I watched the confidence of her steps, the beauty of her legs. Leaves gradually lose their chlorophyll as they grow all year, the guide told us, but the process speeds up toward autumn, and it is loss and decline that leads to such a final explosion of beauty. A flush of colour worth watching just before they fall, a sudden becoming of what they truly are.

Did you know, the guide asked, that this process is called senescence?

It has become one of those fine weeks in mid-September, the leaves finally changing. Orville notices that the world suddenly has a fully autumnal look about it, the very nature of the light giving bushes and houses and cars a golden aspect that seems sharper because it's less bright — objects don't exude light as they did in high summer but, rather, seem to be framed by it

— yet the weather, in the mid twenties, could be summer. The heat gives the autumn scene a sort of distance, the sense that it has been frozen, that time has become moored, like an insect embalmed in amber. Orville hasn't felt this way in years. Autumn has the feeling of hope rather than conclusion.

It takes a moment, as it always does on days with this much warmth and sunlight, not just for his eyes to adjust to the much darker lobby, but for body and spirit to adjust to a shift to the suddenly lower temperature of the air-conditioned room, to a new soundscape, the whisper of papers, click and buzz of phones and front-desk printer, the coughing and mumbling of the half-dozen patients sitting in the chairs. But there is something else, something not generic about the atmosphere today. Some deeper part of his brain knows it before it can be articulated by his conscious mind, always late to the party.

Something is wrong. Rebecca is wearing a light sweater on top of her shirt, the room significantly cooler than outside. Her head is tilted down toward the computer. As usual, she is not looking at him, makes a point of looking only when he stands at the desk (sometimes she makes a show of finishing a task first) and then deals with him politely. But in this case, it's the way she's acting that seems off. She isn't pretending to avoid his eyes as a matter of decorum, to mask their relationship. She seems actually to be evading eye contact, as though put off in some way. Has he offended her recently? Has he not called her enough? Has he made some breach of etiquette, the code he is still learning, youth still a country whose language and customs are only superficially like his own? But, no, that's not it. She's not angry. Her eyes, even as she continues to fumble with a stapler, to glance at her computer, are red.

Good morning. He tries to say it brightly, but it comes out as uncertain.

Good morning, she says. You're all set. Go ahead and take a seat.

It isn't right. This isn't pretend. He looks around. The waiting patients are far enough away to risk a question.

Rebecca, what's wrong?

She shakes her head. She looks like she is going to cry in earnest. The head nurse, Elizabeth, the one who leads Orville into the exam room each week, comes out through the double doors that lead to the exam rooms, walks behind the desk, drops off a form in a tray in front of Rebecca.

Everything okay? Elizabeth asks. She is looking hard at Rebecca.

Rebecca nods. I was just checking Mr Scott in, she says.

Why don't you take a break, Elizabeth says. It's 10.30 — you haven't had one yet, have you? I'll have someone cover the desk for twenty minutes.

Rebecca nods again. She gives Orville a quick look (is it furtive?), then gathers her purse and walks out of the clinic doors.

Okay, Orville, Elizabeth says. Have a seat. We'll be with you in a few minutes.

He looks at the doors Rebecca's gone though. If he leaves through them now, he'd raise the nurse's suspicions. But more than risk her suspecting that Rebecca and he know each other beyond the weekly clinic visits, he has the sense it would in some way get Rebecca into further trouble. He sits down and watches the desk. Elizabeth takes the front desk herself, checks in the few people who walk in. She herself looks in some way worried, her lips pursed. Why does he have the sense that she is guarding the office?

After twenty minutes, Rebecca returns more composed, her eyes dry. She takes Elizabeth's place at the front desk. Elizabeth examines her closely. She seems satisfied, returns to the back. Rebecca studiously avoids his eyes.

Orville? Elizabeth calls a few minutes later, holding open the double doors.

He gets up and follow the nurse into the depths of the clinic to take his medicine.

I suppose marriage, like the sonata, is too easy to harden into some sort of formula. It is easy at the start to think of it as a kind of form, to imagine its movements, to expect certain gestures, expositions, complications, returns. But it's all improvisation. Even with the notes in front of you, wholly constructed, Talia once explained to me about performance, you still interpret, adjust. Two people play the same score in different ways. Even the same pianist, if she is good enough, never plays the same score twice in exactly the same way. Beethoven has laid it all out for you and yet, with all the notations as clear as they could be, you still have to interpret his heart. Is there, in fact, any such thing as music apart from its performance? And with two people improvising, with hardly a note of direction, there is no way to anticipate. It is all fantasy. I think of what Charles Rosen said of the sonata (as quoted by Talia in her manuscript), that it is 'a feeling for proportion, direction, and texture rather than a pattern'. Here, too, there is no ghost structure, no architecture. You build it as you go, and so there are rooms you find you didn't anticipate needing, rooms you built which stand empty, unused, testament to arrogance, which is fundamental to any plan. You fill those rooms with things you don't need or didn't think you wanted. Eventually, two people can be in that large house and avoid each other for days or weeks or whole seasons.

Look, Talia would say if she could read these thoughts, at how you've switched metaphors at your convenience.

This morning, at my dresser picking up the wallet and keys I'd left by habit on top, I see that the glue on one of the yellow sticky notes has finally given in to time and gravity. The note has dropped down from the wall, probably behind the dresser, the other two no doubt to follow soon. I shift the dresser slightly and look behind. It's there, as is a fourth, which must have fallen shortly after she pressed them to the wall.

When I pull the dresser further forward, I see the one just fallen, with the message to herself about 'mainly' loving me, but the one beside it is, to my surprise, one of our notes-on-notes, a 'G' on its stave. Could it possibly be from all of those years ago? I can't imagine how. But no, the musical note is penned on the side with the glue, meant to face the wall. I turn it over. It does have one of her messages to herself, in the wry spirit of the others: *Keep these on the wall; your husband is not as observant as you are.* I turn over the other I'd recovered from behind the dresser. It, too, has a note, an 'F'. *Not as observant:* Of course. A strange sensation, familiar, in my stomach. Not excitement exactly. Anticipation, though not necessarily of the pleasant variety. I lift the next one from the wall and turn it over: Another 'F' note in Talia's familiar writing, neatly drawn if seen from a distance, though on closer inspection slightly smudged. I hesitate only briefly before pulling the last from the wall and turning it over: 'E'. G-F-F-E. Had she toward the end of her period of lucidity still had it in her to play that old familiar game? *Geoff.*

By the time he leaves the clinic, Rebecca's gone for lunch. His phone rings. When he puts it to his ear, she says, Don't say my name. I'll meet you at your house.

When he gets home, Rebecca is sitting on the stoop. He drops his bike on the lawn, sits next to her. This time, it's clear she has just been crying.

She says, If they find out I've been talking to you, I

don't know what they'll do. I can't even risk texts.

Who? Elizabeth?

Elizabeth, yes. Dr Montgomery, too.

You're worried they'll fire you. Do they suspect? I'll say it was my fault.

No, it's not that.

Rebecca, what's going on?

She takes a deep breath. We're in trouble.

Trouble?

The trial might have to shut down. They're telling me to stay quiet while they figure out how to handle this.

Did they threaten you?

Not exactly. But it was, sort of, implied.

What's the problem? Why not just be upfront?

Something's wrong. They haven't told me, but I get the feeling that they've done something wrong, something unofficial. I heard them talking. I don't know.

If something's going wrong, how are they going to keep all of us quiet? An entire trial of people?

Orville, it's just you and Reg. You didn't know that?

Orville lets this sink in. Just two people? He'll need to speak with Alex, at the university. It was his work that started this. He'd said it was an entire trial.

If you don't go back in, they'll suspect something. They'll know I said something, Please. Until we can figure this out.

You want me to go back in there? Get another dose before I even know when they'll shut down or what that will mean for me?

Rebecca says, It's still going on. They said it's still

business as usual. At least for now. But if you don't go back in . . .

What had he been thinking? He'd gotten himself into this. Orville takes her hand, pulls her close for a minute. It's a gorgeous day, oddly as striking to him as it had been only an hour before. Nothing has changed. Everything has.

Michael spoke with me once about recordings. It must have been during our New York trip, when the idea of recording the sonatas was in the works and on his mind, when he was trying to come around to committing to that project, asking himself whether it was the right investment at this point in his career. He said classical recordings are strange animals.

Listeners imagine that these recordings are authentic in the sense of being like performances, he said.

Aren't they, I asked.

Of course not, he said. Think about it. Hit a wrong note in a performance and the mistake, if noticed at all, is quickly forgotten, like clearing a throat in the middle of a conversation or choosing the wrong word or interposing two names — we forgive it. But in a recording, we hear it over and over. So a recording of, say, Beethoven might require a number of splices, replacing a mistake with what we prefer to hear. The recording is meant to provide an experience for the listener, not be a reproduction of some perfect performance by the pianist. The spliced piece might be performed the same day or months later in a different location. Then of course there are issues to do with microphone placement and other tricks of sound engineering. The thing is, this is also true when we record concert performances. So we can use words like fidelity, but there's nothing truly faithful about a recording, at least not to some ideal of performance. If it's faithful to anything, it is not to what happened but to what we want to hear. Fidelity is a matter less of truth to memory or intention than of getting the story straight.

Orville has always enjoyed walking through the university campus, a sprawling 500-acre mix of buildings and green spaces that would be a peaceful place if it were not constantly in a state of construction. It had gotten a new president nearly a decade before, and he'd gone on a building spree that included a new recreation centre, new student centre, an IT building, two large parking garages, three dorms and a beautiful new administration building. He'd also doubled the size of the law school. All of this had both stemmed from alumni donations and sparked more alumni donations, since alumni like to be part of something on the way up. As Orville walks across campus from one of the new parking structures — built at the far east end — he passes yet another building under construction, though he has no idea what it is meant to become.

The science tower, though, remains as it has been for years. Orville doesn't know whether this is by design — whether the president is purposefully neglecting the hard sciences — or whether, as is more likely, he simply hasn't gotten around to the expensive project of replacing one of the modernist monstrosities on campus. Orville takes the elevator to the eighth floor and walks down the hall, the cinderblock walls occasionally covered with student or faculty conference posters. Alex's door is slightly ajar.

Orville knocks perfunctorily then opens it. Alex is kneeling by a filing cabinet, the bottom drawer open. He is putting files into a cardboard box. He looks up.

Can I help you?

Orville hasn't seen Alex in months, but he'd assumed that Alex has been following the trial, that he's been seeing the photographs and videos taken each time Orville went for treatment.

Alex, it's me, Orville.

Alex stares, slowly standing, a file in his hand.

Orville, my god, Alex says.

I know.

You're a different person.

I'm the same person. Haven't you seen the pictures?

Alex blushes. I've been following things, he says, but it's one thing to see a picture, another to see it in the flesh.

He's lying. Orville can tell that.

Alex, what's going on?

I don't know what you mean, Alex says. When he speaks he opens the file, keeping his eyes on that, not on Orville.

Alex, Orville says, why haven't you been following your own trial?

Alex looks back up at him. From the start of their

friendship, Orville has seen him as a younger man. But what Orville is discovering, as he grows younger himself, is that his perceptions of age are changing. Just as people in their twenties and thirties began to look very young — even the same — as Orville had grown older, and older people began to become more differentiated as individuals, the reverse has started to occur. He finds himself seeing older people as more uniform, as elderly. A man of Alex's age — in his fifties — now seems much older to him. His brain was behind his body, but it is catching up.

Alex says, It's just that the pictures don't do you justice.

You're not telling me the truth. Something's happening. I've learned the trial is shutting down.

Who told you that?

It doesn't matter. I got into this through you. You've clearly not seen the photographs, so please no bullshit. What is going on?

I don't know what you mean.

I'm not leaving until you tell me.

Alex lets out a breath and sits down in his desk chair.

Okay, Alex says, I'll explain everything. Then I'm going to leave for a while, with all of these notes. And I recommend you leave, too.

Anna took Talia for a walk to give me some peace and has just returned her. Talia is in her room, resting, perhaps asleep. Anna has for once accepted a cup of tea, which we drink at the kitchen table, my notes and computer pushed to the side.

I suppose I am quiet for too long because Anna asks, What are you thinking?

And so I tell her. I tell her that I consider that period our two families spent without each other's company, as our two sons grew up and we grew older only a few miles apart, to be lost years. I try to reassure her. I say I understand that raising Bede was all-consuming, that their social circle would inevitably be dominated by his needs, that we were in different parenting places, but that I am glad they came back to us.

But it wasn't that way at all, Anna says.

What do you mean?

I wanted to keep you in the loop on Bede. I wanted you to see him grow, to be a presence in his life. It was you who withdrew.

She stares into her tea, then directly into my eyes. It was you.

What I never expected to emerge from the course of Talia's illness was the sense of losing my own history. Hers, of course. I expected her sense of self to dissipate — though I dreaded it — along with her memory of her profession, her conversations with her sister, her desires and rages. I expected her to forget the way we used to sit out on the deck and watch rain clouds thicken, feel the humidity gather in the air, wait with eyes closed as the first drops splashed on our skins before running into the house, a regular event when we were younger (at what point had it become history?). To lose my wife's knowledge of who I am — that is in a very real way to lose the knowledge myself. There is no one left alive who knows as much about me, both from the recollections I've shared with her (*Recollected too often*, she said) and the length of the journey taken together. What I know of myself is informed, even constructed, by her wry responses and reflections, the occasional admissions of affection, even admiration. That is the oddest, though not the most important, part of losing her, even as she sits just a few feet away.

There is a section in Talia's book where she discusses debates over Beethoven's own views about extraneous material in his music — noting one observer (and she goes back to a 1911 source here) who argues that 'extraneous ideas had struck him as magnificent material for instrumental music.' Talia is nothing if not thorough. She even quotes a Florida State University doctoral thesis — *A Structural-Aesthetic Study of the Variation Movements of Beethoven's Late Period* — to make her point about such extraneous material, specifically that 'temporal disjunctions set apart passages of dramatically contrasting musical material that may at first seem extraneous but often carry a structural function. In the same way, formal insertions such as episodes may contribute to the underlying tonal or aesthetic structure.' How much of our lives is the extraneous material that acts as its scaffolding, which is not part of the edifice but is a necessary support structure for its construction and its decoration? Who is to say whether what is extraneous is inextricable from the very process that produced what was most relevant?

In all the years since that summer, Anna and I have never talked about it. Not when she became pregnant — against the odds, the doctor said. Certainly not when she came to our house with Geoff, who seemed so proud, so relieved to be having a child, that it suggested to me just how hard the years without success had been for him, so much harder than I gave him credit for. He'd worked at the nonchalance I'd associated with so many of those years, and contrary to my uncharitable speculations at the time it was simply a manifestation of his desire to have his own child, his refusal to give up. It was a boy, they'd told us. They said they'd told themselves they wanted a surprise but when they got the ultrasound, they couldn't wait to know. I go back over my memory of their announcement: Thanksgiving day. Michael had a blessed day off from his life. He was busier than any boy should be, shuttling endlessly from school to piano to homework to more piano. Since the start of school, he'd no longer had time for his endless disappearances. I wondered about Lewis, who never came to the house and whose name Michael didn't mention anymore. Geoff and Anna had come by for dinner. They brought a pie — was it apple? — and ice cream. The day was mainly grey throughout the morning, but the afternoon brought a hint of sunshine, the weak late-autumn variety. It had already become very cold, waves of chill underneath the central heat, our windows draughty. Still, I had turned on all the lights to give the house a sense of warmth, had loaded up the fireplace and put out some candles. The lights, the fire, the smell of the food in the oven, all of it gave the house a cosiness, an under-your-skin warmth it seemed to me it hadn't had in a long time. And then they showed up with their pie, their ice cream, a can of artificial whipped cream, and with a bottle of what I took to be the champagne that had become the traditional way for us to toast in what Geoff called the silly season. I managed to squeeze the pie onto the counter, filled with side dishes and dirty dishes and serving platters. When I immediately went to open the bottle and read the label — by habit — I found that it was sparkling grape juice. I looked at it and then looked to Talia, pointed it out to her. She got it faster than I did. Her eyes widened. She held up the bottle and looked at them.

Are you telling me . . .?

Anna barely had time to nod before Talia embraced her.

I poured it into the set of four champagne glasses we'd received from Anna and Geoff for our wedding. Anna and Talia broke their long embrace. Geoff looked me in the eye and shook my hand. When I turned to her, Anna sipped her juice and looked elsewhere.

By the time Orville leaves his office, Alex is in tears. He'd explained it all. To fund his research, Alex had gone into partnership with a start-up that in turn had received funding from a venture capital company. The start-up had insisted on separating Alex's involvement from the trial itself, bringing in its own professionals once Alex had set up the relationship with the clinic. Alex had gradually been shut out of the trial, promised only that he would get the results and share in publication, as well as in any commercial application — all of which he had come seriously to doubt.

Why, Orville asked, is the trial shutting down?

Alex looked away then. Side effects, I gather. They won't give me the details.

Side effects? I haven't felt anything.

Not you. The other participant.

You mean Reg? What sort of side effects, Alex?

Alex swore that he didn't know. He only knew that they had decided to stop the trial and that all records were to be taken away and destroyed.

They can't destroy records. There are reports about these sorts of thing, aren't there? Sent to health officials or some such?

Alex shook his head. Not everything has gone according to protocol, he said. I lost control of this a long time ago.

Doesn't the FDA have protocols . . .

Have you ever heard of a two-person FDA-approved trial?

Are you saying . . .

The FDA doesn't know about this.

Orville was stunned. But why . . .?

The money, Alex said.

You didn't say anything to me. You could have called me.

Alex put his hands to face, rubbed his head. I'm scared of these people, Orville.

At least you were looking out for yourself.

And you weren't? Look at you. You knew there would be risks, and look at what you've gotten. A new body, a new lifetime.

If I survive this. If I don't show signs of whatever it is that happened to Reg.

I asked, Orville. I did that. There have been no signs of any problem with you.

No signs for now, Orville said. They could still occur.

They could. But if they haven't so far, something's different.

What? Why am I being spared?

Alex said, It might have to do with your chemotherapy.

Orville was too surprised to speak.

Yes, Alex said, I know about it.

You didn't say . . .

I didn't know at the time. But when they started to talk about side effects, I looked into both sets of medical records more carefully. I did a bit more investigating.

And you think that's why.

I don't know. They won't give me the records they've kept on you, all those weeks of poking and prodding you. They're getting rid of it all. It's just a factor. It's something that differentiates you in a significant way from Reg. It could be something else.

I'm sorry I didn't tell you.

No, you're not. You wanted this. For whatever reason, you were willing to take a risk on this experiment, and you were willing to take the extra risk of lying about your medical history.

What are you saying?

I'm saying that you're not an innocent victim here. You wanted this, would do anything to go back. You wanted to be young again. Maybe you should ask yourself why.

Maybe I should. But this isn't the way it is supposed to work at all. For once, I am writing a story meant to take me away from introspection, to get me away from myself, not turn me inwards.

I know Geoff's book is on my shelf, but it takes me twenty minutes to locate it. My shelves have a general order about them, but I'm lazy about re-shelving, inclined to place books where it is convenient. When she had her wits about her, Talia would have found a book on her shelves with hardly a moment's thought. I do find it, though, tucked two rows over from its home, and search it. Yes, a section on memory. He quotes Schacter — that's the name:

We now know that we do not record our experiences the way a camera records them. Our memories work differently. We extract key elements form our experiences and store them. We then recreate or reconstruct rather than retrieve copies of them. Sometimes, in the process of reconstructing we add on feelings, beliefs, or even knowledge we obtained after the experience.

Pencilled in the margins, in my handwriting, is a notation: 'See A.V. Chandrha, Disorder, 87.' This time it takes only a moment to lay my hands on it, Chandra's novel, *Dwelling in Disorder*, which I'd read some years before. I turn to p. 87, where I find a section of dialogue bracketed in pencil, marked with an asterisk. The main character is a cab driver in New York, but he was formerly a doctor in Pakistan. He is having a conversation, via his rear-view mirror, with a passenger who insists that they are driving in the wrong direction, that he'd made this drive only a year earlier in another cab and was certain he knew the way. The cabbie laughs. 'I don't doubt it. But what of it? When we remember something, it is not just that we slash a new path through the jungle. It is not even the same jungle.'

Let's call this Variation 1:
Michael leaves our home, this much I know. I know he is upset, that he has left abruptly, hardly saying goodbye after a weekend visit, a weekend of pouring

rain outside and cups of coffee inside (I made them, he drank them). He spent much of that time helping Talia with her manuscript, tracking down notes, working with her on some thoughts about the sonatas. I wander through the living room now and again, where they are at the table or sometimes the piano. Sometimes it's just Michael at the piano, Talia watching him from the table or the couch. Sometimes they sit together. The work is going slowly, casually; the real reason he has come is simply to spend time with her. A year ago now when Talia had more periods of clarity. Still, she would forget details, confuse events, repeat herself. She seemed buffeted by neurological waves. A wave would pass through, she would get confused, then she would return. I could tell it was disturbing to Michael, though he tried not to show it, had learned to keep the smile on his face as one of those waves passed.

The question is the cause. Why did he leave the house so abruptly the last time we saw him? I try to put myself in Michael's mind, behind his eyes. He's tired, having come here to help Talia, not just with her manuscript but help her to feel normal, to have a sense of connection to the son she misses so terribly, to the work, and to the world to which that work is a bridge, a bridge extending farther each day so that no matter how many miles she travels, the next day she finds that she is even farther from that world, the world of her mind to which she wants to return. But I'm in Talia's mind now, not Michael's, so hard to get into his, always has been. He sees his mother, her hands jittery, a sense of uncertainty about her, an uncertainty that rises from the gaps, those waves that run through her, a sense that she might be saying what she has already said or that she has forgotten something important that she wanted to say or needed to do, a pot on the stove or an unlatched window or a page needing correction. I'm in her head again. Back to Michael's: He sees these waves come through, the jittery motions of her hands that have always held so steady, have been the very steadiness of his life, sees the mess of the notes and articles she means to use to complete her book, his mother always so organised, who taught him the discipline he has taken on, the crisp ironed collars of his shirts, the tidy arrangement of his own books, the potential chaos of his life — with its concerts and recordings and practices and interviews — brought to order, made possible, by the very discipline she taught him, those very principles slipping away from her. He sees her hands shake, her smile waver. He works with her on a piece to help her get inside it as he would. She can still play and, though she is at her best, most like herself, at the keys, as a son and as a professional he can tell the difference. It is this very difference, a difference so subtle that it is not evident to someone outside of those twin intimacies — with her as a mother, with her as a pianist — so much more subtle than the manifestations of her gradual decline in other ways, that bothers him most. In fact, it is these that make him most angry, and her apologies for minor errors anger him further, anger him for reasons he can't possibly articulate or defend (his mother, his fierce protector, now abandoning him and the music that made for their intimacy) because he knows such reasoning is indefensible — purely human but indefensible no less, an anger that, despite his efforts, she senses is directed at her, which brings tears to her eyes, tears she had until now always, no matter how hurt he had made her in the past, as a teenager or beyond, been able to hide but no longer has the control to hide, tears that do nothing but further inflame his anger until he has to get up, stalk away, leave, his anger now at himself, at his own weakness, as if he were a teenager again, turning away from her. He slams the door, needs to cool off, walks through the rain without his jacket, gets into his rental car so that when I return from the kitchen with a slice of cake and a fresh cup of coffee to the sound of the slammed door he is gone and Talia is sitting at the piano bench lost.

Variation 2:
Michael is exhausted after three months of touring and after only a few days with Jacob in New York comes to help Talia, ostensibly to help her get inside the music, to show her the challenges, the struggles of getting inside the sonata, not just the technical issues but the emotional ones, though he's really there to observe, to see how far his mother has gone from him, and also to . . . what? Observe me? Could it be me that he was observing as much as his mother? For what? To see if I am capable of holding up my end, of getting her to take her meds, of keeping my own needs second in the queue, as I've not been capable of

doing in the past? What does he see? An old man. A man his mother has called selfish too many times to count, enough times over the years to get that notion into Michael's head, to be a shape of my character that he feels he has observed himself rather than one that has been drawn for him. An old man hovering at the edges of the scene doing useless things like making a cup of coffee for his son in one of those French presses, placing it on the table — when did his father's hands start to do that tremble, Michael will ask himself — a cup of coffee that instead Talia picks up, spills not over herself thank god; we are spared the burns, but it spills over the papers they are trying to organise: *What are you thinking, Dad, leaving it within reach.* This old man in his out-of-fashion baggy khakis and his twenty-year-old rag wool sweater and his glasses that he forgets on the side table or by the mail on the entry table or perched on his own head — not Alzheimer's, just the frustrating new normal that time accords — a man who has taken to using a hearing aid whose settings are challenging to calibrate so that voices are loud enough but background noise not overwhelming, who is rarely sitting still with his wife or talking with his son but always vacuuming or doing dishes or taking out rubbish or writing his book or doing some other postpone-able task in some other room. Yes, this is perhaps the source of Michael's anger: not the mother and her frailties but the father who has never quite measured up in the eyes of the mother, which became the eyes of the son who can't see for all his intelligence that what he takes for observation is verbal recollection. Or is that an old man's wishful thinking. Is this father in fact that stooped, ingratiating figure, selfishness hard-wired, a character trait still apparent even in the face of his wife's needs. Not needs but the singular need, encompassing all others: the need to be secure. How the father thinks now of that hawk, how it flew through a summer of their lives. What might the boy have observed that they'd assumed he hadn't, he wonders. He thinks of that bird, its essential wildness, the way that wildness, fleeting as it was, connected them all to something less rooted in the domestic, their own domestication threatening to fall apart, held together by a few piano notes, a child to take care of, a force of will. It might not stand out in Michael's mind at all. Our obsessions rarely duplicate themselves in the minds of others, even those we assume affected. Why so angry then? Why would this — elderly, is that the adjective, can it possibly apply — man, the fact that he hovers so uselessly, or fails to hover often enough, be sufficient to cause Michael — who when I left the room to get him something to eat had been concentrating so deeply on his work with Talia, had been sitting next to her listening to her play, had been reading a file — suddenly to say he needs space, to slam the door, to get into his rental car, which the old man comes into the room in time to see pull away from the curb, sees it through the living room window, watches it pull into the wet street, the belated signal as it turns right, the final glimpse of its slick, black exterior as it drops down the hill toward town.

Variation 3:

Michael is exhausted, harried, doesn't want to be there but has to be there, wants to see his mother but doesn't want to see her because it is too painful. He is working with Talia on her papers, giving her his sense of what it is to be inside that music she knows so well, but not in the way he does. His is the double-commitment to his mother the writer, his mother the Alzheimer's patient. Talia calls out something to her husband, some piece of critique. And Michael gets angry. Angry at her for criticising him, as she has done a thousand times before in his presence? No, nor angry about the truth underlying the criticism: not her critique itself but his father's passive acceptance of it. Does this figure his son regards truly look stooped, small, still intimidated by his own wife after so many years? Is it anger at that history and what it taught Michael, not to become that very thing? Hence the source of his anger is not the moment's trigger, her critique, but rather a life-long resistance to that kernel of himself he has learned from this ageing figure? I can't remember what she might have said to me. But was it enough to trigger him in light of the pressures of that house? The summer the hawk flew through our lives was my last sort of youthful resistance to Talia's authority. It was too hard. My rebellions after that were much smaller, quieter, subtler — so subtle she hardly knew they existed, hardly rebellions at all. The sound of the piano that morning and most of the afternoon, there and not there, Michael showing a passage to Talia, explaining how he was inside of it, Talia giving it a try. That sonata, Op. 109, playing over and over in the house: Was the anger in the music or in Michael's hands? Was it that the anger in the music grew in the context of that house, became too powerful to be contained by the form? That it blossomed from the keys into his fingers and through Michael's body until he slammed the top of the piano with his open palm and then the door so hard the vibrations caused the painting in the entry hall to slip on its wire so that it hung leaning to the right, the father's eye drawn to the painting first, its strange angle something that he understood intuitively before realising what was wrong with its position, then to the open window as the black sedan Michael had rented put on its belated signal and disappeared?

Variation 4:

The painting is like so many pieces of art in one's own home, nearly invisible after a while, forgotten until remarked on by a visitor or until you have to straighten it after your son slams the door so hard it shifts on its wire. Anna and Geoff gave it to us, so many years ago now. An anniversary gift, I think, something they'd picked up on a trip. A woman, not quite realistic, not quite impressionistic, staring not directly at the viewer but to the side, as though distracted by something through the window behind the painter, or perhaps just bored, or maybe she doesn't like the painter or is thinking about what she will do when she has fulfilled this commitment and received payment. Her hair is dark, curly, her hands in her lap. That's right, they had taken a trip to the Sunshine Coast, the big trip to Australia. Anna was finally pregnant, they were cocooning, but first a trip to the beach, and it was there, in some gallery, they found this painting and bought it for us. It's not a contemporary setting, exactly; something early century. The woman in the painting seemed older when they gave it to us — I remember thinking she was someone's grandmother. But I've caught up and passed her now, and she strikes me as young, maybe in her fifties. I remember they looked good, had clearly gotten some sun, had that vacation glow. Geoff looked so excited — I hadn't seen him so visibly excited. Anna, very pregnant — she gave birth nine weeks later, a week early — beside him, mainly talking to Talia. A few looks at me. No, away from me. No, the woman in the painting is not bored. Restless. That's different. There is something in her gaze past the painter — past us — that suggests she wants something, yearns for something. No, realises something. A look of concern on her face, as though in thinking about what she hopes for she has suddenly realised the extent of some obstacle to that fulfillment. She's remembering something. Forever remembering and we can only guess at what sits just on the other side of her gaze, what concern she holds, whether she overcame that obstacle. Crooked on its wire after Michael slammed that door. It was like I was seeing it for the first time. Things can get so familiar we no longer see them. I watched from the window as he drove away.

Variation 5:

Michael is asking how long this can go on.

I say, What do you mean go on, what else is there to do but go on?

Michael says, You know what I mean, Dad.

I don't, Michael, what else to do but go on while she needs me?

That is not what I mean by go on, Dad. No one is saying you're not taking care of her or shouldn't.

So what are you saying, what shouldn't go on?

Sometimes I think you are the one with the problem, he says, not her.

I have a lot of problems.

Right, avoid this.

Look, how can you say I am avoiding anything? I'm dealing every day with your mother's memory problems.

Hers are inevitable, Michael says, but your memory problems are purposeful.

Tell me about these problems.

How you won't look at reality, Dad.

What reality would that be, Michael? It all feels pretty real here.

Real in what sense, Dad?

Your mother, her dementia, getting up at all hours when I hear her because I'm afraid she'll wander off again and often does. Is that not real enough for you, Michael?

For god's sake, Dad, that's real, it's just a bracketed reality, a piece of reality you're focusing on.

Michael, why don't you just tell me what you mean

instead of talking around it, instead of being coy: Why don't you just go ahead and lay out the contours of this reality that seems to be bothering you so much. Why don't you just talk to me instead of offering these little critiques that I need to interpret, like little snatches of song, a tune I have to follow in all of its permutations.

Yes, Dad, permutations is a good word, a word that suggests perhaps you do know what I mean, that at some level you are aware of these realities, of your role in them, not just hers but your own. Why can't you admit to yourself the truth?

Is this truth what makes you so angry, Michael, so angry that you need to slam the piano, slam the door, drive away?

Wouldn't you be angry, Dad, if you discovered the truth and all that you had been hiding, most of all from yourself?

Is that what I've been doing, hiding it from myself?

Yes, Dad, hiding it from yourself, from me.

And your mother?

Leave Mum out of this, Dad. This is about you. This is about acknowledging reality.

Okay, Michael, let's acknowledge the truth. Go ahead, state the truth.

No, Dad, you need to say it.

Why, Michael, if you are so angry, why won't you say it?

Because I'm not here, Dad. I've already left. I drove away, you never saw me again. I'm gone, except this last place, a voice in your head, a tune that won't let you alone, an ear worm you can't dislodge.

I will never dislodge you, but do we have to see it all straight on — is it necessary to face, yes, the music, Dad, that's exactly right.

So we reach The Final Variation. This is the one I least want to plumb. This is the version where I have to admit to the Michael-in-my-head, the only Michael I will ever have to speak with again, that I know it is not that he is angry at me for my passivity before Talia, nor at his mother for her dementia, not exactly, nothing so childish. This is the version where Michael is helping her to go through her notes, when he discovers the same note to herself that I did, 'check op. cit., 109 file'. The version where he follows the same pathway that I did to her files — the file is probably on the desk there near the piano, so he does not have to go into her filing cabinet — and discovers that folded piece of paper with handwriting that is not his mother's, the letter written on stationery from Hotel Gerrard. Would he know the date of the concert where she played Op. 109? Of course he would. He would at some point early in her writing of this book or perhaps earlier than that — during his own preparations for the recordings of the sonatas — have had a discussion with Talia about her own experiences playing it, her own interpretations and challenges. His greatest confidante on all things musical, his mother. Michael could do the simple math as well as I could. Imagine the calculation, the impossible sum, the question to which it gives rise and the seemingly inevitable answer. He would have assumed that I knew, too, though I didn't because I had not yet discovered it. He would have been furious at his mother and even angrier that in her current mental state he couldn't confront her, demand an explanation. And furious at me for the withholding I had not yet done. Of course he would have been at a loss for how to contain those feelings and would have left to at least clear his head. Would he have returned a few minutes, an hour or two later, to confront me and discuss it? I think so. But I can't know because every variation ends the same way: He hits another car head-on — the rain, his impossible emotional state — then we never see Michael again, Talia lets go of her tentative grip on the sill over the depths of her Alzheimer's, I read about Beethoven in the last book she will publish and I write about Orville in a story I will never finish. Best to abandon it as a necessary structural extraneity. *Your little redemption fantasies.* No, sooner or later, Orville will discover that there is no going back. He is just going forward in a younger body. Those drives he had will be more intense, again. He will be just as helpless before them. Of course things would go wrong for Orville. There is no do-over, only a new path and the same obstacles. Let him make those same mistakes without me. Give me the strength to face my own.

Any sense of redemption is here, today, from this moment, late as it is. The sun is close to the hills now. I've helped Talia to her piano stool. Her fingers reach for the keys — still that instinct remains — and I am easily forgotten. I slip away and, the neighbours be damned, stand outside my own window, in my own front yard, to watch her like the stranger I was all of those years ago and have become for her again. Listen to Sonata No. 30 in E Major, Op. 109. Really listen to it. If you can get someone you once loved to play it, you might really hear it. The window is half-open, the music she makes consuming all of my attention, I suppose, which must explain why I was deaf to the crunch of tyres as the car pulled up, to the soft friction of feet through the grass. It doesn't pay to imagine the aged figure they saw as they approached me. I become aware only when I see the reflection appear behind me in the glass of the window — his reflection: older but his face still square, his build still slight. And, standing behind him, back at the lawn's edge, a face so familiar I know its every ageing, beautiful contour. Anna's, his mother's. I know I have to turn around. But I let that moment hold, like a lingering note, before I face him. Not Michael, never again. But still, my son.

Acknowledgements

The idea for a book centered on Sonata No. 30, Op. 109 was inspired by a free online course I took some years ago on Beethoven's sonatas through Coursera and the Curtis Institute of Music, with engaging lectures by the pianist Jonathan Biss. Many thanks to Mr Biss, who as I recall used the term "Russian doll" with regard to the sonata's final movement—I remain a grateful "Courserian." Recollection can of course be unreliable, hence the notion that each visit to a memory is not just a new path through the jungle but a new jungle, a comment made to me once by my old friend Donald B. Katz, a neuroscientist and professor at Brandeis. I enjoyed reading about life as a professional pianist in Charles Rosen's *Piano Notes*, from which I gleaned insights about splicing and fidelity that Michael explains to Stephen; my direct quotation from Rosen on the sonata as a "feeling for proportion" can be found in his book *Sonata Forms*. Stephen's reference to Schacter on memory refers to Daniel L. Schacter and can be found in his book *The Seven Sins of Memory: How the Mind Forgets and Remembers*.

The doctoral thesis I briefly quote—"A Structural-Aesthetic Study of the Variation Movements of Beethoven's Late Period"—is by Judith Ofcarcik, issued in 2013 and held in the Florida State University Libraries. The reference to the 1911 source on extraneous material is from the 1911 *Encyclopædia Britannica*, reproduced on Wikisource. References to the past as a foreign country allude to the opening of the novel *The Go-Between* by L.P. Hartley: 'The past is a foreign country; they do things differently there.' The epigraph of the novella is an instruction to performers by Beethoven at the start of the sonata's third movement; it has been translated variously, and I found this version in an explanation on the Hyperion Records website, attributed to Barry Cooper. Many thanks to the pianist Ludwig Treviranus in Auckland for answering my questions (though any errors are mine), for taking me to a house concert of Op. 109, and for being such an engaged piano teacher for our children. My appreciation to Massey University's College of Humanities and Social Sciences, and the School of English & Media Studies, for some time to complete the book. Thanks, too, to Alice Grundy for choosing this novella for Seizure and for her careful and incisive editing. Thanks to Arthur Golubiewski for the hawks. My deepest gratitude as always to my wife, Nancy Golubiewski, for believing in me, and to my children, who must sometimes be reminded to practise but who fill our home, and our hearts, with song.

VIVA
LA NOVELLA

Viva la Novella is an annual prize awarded for short works between twenty and fifty thousand words. Since its beginnings in 2013 the award has published sixteen short novels by sixteen outstanding authors.

For more information, please visit our website
www.seizureonline.com

VIVA LA NOVELLA 2020 WINNERS

Late Sonata by Bryan Walpert
978-1-922267-23-8 (print) | 978-1-922267-24-5 (digital)

Dark Wave by Lana Guineay
978-1-922267-25-2 (print) | 978-1-922267-26-9 (digital)

VIVA LA NOVELLA 2019 WINNERS

Listurbia by Carly Cappielli
978-1-925589-87-0 (print) | 978-1-925589-88-7 (digital)

Offshore by Joshua Mostafa
978-1-925589-89-4 (print) | 978-1-925589-90-0 (digital)

VIVA LA NOVELLA 2018 WINNERS

Swim by Avi Duckor-Jones
978-1-925589-50-4 (print) | 978-1-925589-51-1 (digital)

The Bed-Making Competition by Anna Jackson
978-1-925589-52-8 (print) | 978-1-925589-53-5 (digital)

Available online and from discerning book retailers